Books by Natalie Babbitt

Dick Foote and the Shark
Phoebe's Revolt
The Search for Delicious
Kneeknock Rise
The Something
Goody Hall
The Devil's Storybook
Tuck Everlasting
The Eyes of the Amaryllis
Herbert Rowbarge
The Devil's Other Storybook
Nellie: A Cat on Her Own
Bub, or The Very Best Thing
Ouch!
Elsie Times Eight

Goody Hall

STORY AND PICTURES

BY NATALIE BABBITT

SQUARE
FISH

FARRAR, STRAUS AND GIROUX

**SQUARE
FISH**

An Imprint of Holtzbrinck Publishers

Square Fish and the Square Fish logo are trademarks of Holtzbrinck Publishers, LLC and

are used by Farrar, Straus and Giroux under license from Holtzbrinck Publishers, LLC.

Library of Congress Cataloging-in-Publication Data Available
Library of Congress Catalog Card Number: 73-149221

ISBN-13: 978-0-312-36983-5 / ISBN-10: 0-312-36983-2

Originally published in the United States by Farrar, Straus and Giroux
First Square Fish Edition: September 2007
10 9 8 7 6 5 4 3 2 1
www.squarefishbooks.com

"To thine own self renew,

and it must follow, as the knight the doe,

thou canst not then befall to any man."

Hercules Feltwright

For Michael di Capua

Sine Quo Non

Goody Hall

CHAPTER 1

The blacksmith stood in the door of his shop and sniffed the May breeze hopefully. "There's something in the air, no doubt about it," he said to himself with satisfaction. "Something's going to happen." He fixed a pipeful of tobacco and lit it contentedly, sorting over in his mind a number of possibilities. There was the baker's daughter, Millie, who had been in love with the new parson all winter and was said to be pining away because he refused to notice her. Perhaps she would throw herself off the church roof —that would be interesting! There was Alf Hulser's son Fred, who had been jailed for stealing a cow— maybe he would try to escape. And then, wasn't it time for Pooley's barn to catch fire again? It burned to the ground about once every five years. The blacksmith scanned the skies for signs of a storm. Lightning was always good for starting fires. But the sky was clear, so he leaned against the door frame and thought about the last fire. "Five years ago exactly," he nodded to himself, counting back. "One of the best fires we ever had." And it had happened the very day before that rich fellow Midas Goody fell off his horse and killed himself.

"Yoo-hoo there!" called a voice. The blacksmith peered down the street through a cloud of pipe smoke and saw a big, heavy woman dressed in black hurrying toward him. "Good morning, Henry!" she said breathlessly as she came up. "What are you standing out here for? Let's go inside. I've been marketing all morning and I want to rest up before I start back to the Hall."

"Come in then," said the blacksmith, "and tell me the news."

The big woman in the black dress was the blacksmith's sister and her name was Dora Tidings. *Mrs.* Dora Tidings. "A widow—a very respectable widow," the villagers declared, "who supports herself by keeping house for that woman out to Goody Hall. *You* know the place, like a regular palace—if you like palaces. Well, Mrs. Goody's rich, all right, but it takes more than money to make a fine lady, and that poor little boy of hers, cooped up away from natural play and exercise, although they do say he's a regular holy terror. Mrs. Goody hasn't changed her ways one bit since her husband was killed so suddenly that night, and no one ever saw her shed a tear over him. Not that anyone ever knew much about them, coming out of nowhere the way they did—but he was a fine gentleman, you know, or at least that's what Dora Tidings says."

What Dora Tidings said counted for a good deal in the village. She was the only one who could be depended upon to pass along the news about the rich Mrs. Goody and her son, and she enjoyed her impor-

tance so much that she stayed on and on at Goody
Hall, with no one to help her except the gardener's
daughter, Alfreida, who came in afternoons. Not that
gypsies were ever much help, the gossip ran, and
there was certainly gypsy blood in those two somewhere. All right, so maybe they *did* have a cottage all
their own at the edge of the village instead of the
usual gaudy caravan, but still—once a gypsy, always
a gypsy. And, of course, nobody in her right mind
would hire one to do anything, let alone be a house-
maid or a gardener. So there had to be something very
strange about that woman out there and someday, the
villagers said to each other, Dora Tidings would find
out what it was.

"She's got a new bee in her bonnet," said Mrs.
Tidings to her brother the blacksmith as she sank
gratefully onto a nail keg inside the shop. Mrs. Tidings always referred to her employer, Mrs. Goody,
as "she."

"Yes?" said the blacksmith encouragingly.

"Well!" said Mrs. Tidings. "She's decided she
needs a tutor for that boy, Willet. She's taught him

his reading and numbers already, but now she wants him to learn a lot of other things, so she's going to look for a tutor. I asked her—I said, 'Why don't you send that boy to school in the village?' And *she* said she didn't want to do that because Willet wasn't used to having a lot of other children around and they might make things hard for him. But it isn't that, of course. What she's thinking is the village children aren't fancy enough for a Goody."

"Where is she going to find a tutor in these parts?" asked the blacksmith.

"I'm sure *I* don't know," said Mrs. Tidings, looking upward and shaking her head.

"By the way, Dora," said the blacksmith, leaning forward. "Isn't it just five years ago that Midas Goody died? Remember? It was right after Pooley's barn burned down last time."

"I should say I do remember," said Mrs. Tidings. "Yes, five years almost to the day."

"She'll be putting flowers at the tomb, I suppose," said the blacksmith with a sour smile.

Mrs. Tidings folded her lips. "Not her, as you very

well know. Not so much as a petal. Nothing in all the years I've been with her. It certainly is a strange way to behave."

The blacksmith was silent, thinking ahead to his own tomb. He always pictured it heaped with roses and washed on a regular basis by the gentle tears of his own devoted wife. He thought anxiously of that wife for a moment and a small doubt occurred to him that made him even crosser with the mysterious Mrs. Goody. "You're right, Dora," he said. "It certainly is a strange way to behave."

CHAPTER 2

Spring in those long-gone times was exactly like spring today, of course. Some things never change. The birds were just as merry, the grass as tender, and the air had that same exciting lightness which threatened, if you breathed too deeply, to lift you right up off the ground. One morning not long after, a baggy young man came down the road from the village, and in spite of his heavy satchel he half bounced, half glided like a large balloon, gulping great lungfuls of May as a thirsty man gulps water, and letting them out again in blasts of shapeless song. He had been singing all the way from the village, swinging the scuffed old satchel from one hand and gesturing with the other from time to time when he felt the song required it, and his long face was blissful and absorbed.

Just as he reached for the fortieth time a particular place in the music which sounded like "Merrily, merrily shall I live now," but wasn't quite that, somehow, he came to a sudden bend in the road and the song ceased abruptly. "Aha!" said the baggy young man. "This is the place. It must be." And he put down the satchel and went forward.

It was a house that had stopped him, a beautiful house that rose up from its dewy square of barbered lawn like a wedding cake on a green tray—a house so white and frilly with chiseled wooden filigree and balconies, so rich in scalloped eaves and dormers, so decked with slender columns and peaking, bright-tiled roofs that it would have stopped anyone. It was a lacy handkerchief, a valentine, a regular seafoam of a house, and the baggy young man stood quite still in the middle of the road and looked at it for a long time. Then he went up to the gatepost and peered into the square of brass that was fastened there. *Goody Hall*, the square announced in a soft gleam of letters. Yes, that was the name they had given him in the village.

"If it's talking work you want," the blacksmith had said, "they're looking for a tutor out to Goody Hall. It's quite a place. My sister's the housekeeper. Why don't you go along and see about it?" But after the baggy young man had gone, the blacksmith remarked to a friend, "I don't think they'll want the likes of *him*, though. What a queer duck! Not a whisker on him anywhere!" And he stroked his own sooty beard complacently.

To which the friend replied, "Well, they're strange themselves at Goody Hall, aren't they? Fellow like that ought to suit them just right. I don't see why your sister stays on out there year after year."

The blacksmith picked up his hammer. "Oh well,"

he said, smiling modestly into his beard, "she's full of curiosity, you know. Also, the pay is good. But mostly it's curiosity."

"Yes," said the friend, "I can understand that."

But the baggy young man had heard none of this and now he was leaning on the gate and looking at the beautiful house with a sort of hypnotized pleasure. As he stared, his mind's eye squinted and he seemed to see himself coming out of the tall door, a new and polished self in an elegant black suit. He watched this self pause on the verandah, pluck a blossom from a flowering shrub that leaned there, and hold it delicately under his nose. Then the scene enlarged. A crowd of ragged people appeared at the gate, clutching their thin coats under their chins. "There he is!" cried the ragged people. "There he is! Bless you, sir! Bless you!" He saw himself striding down the long gravel path to the gate and now he was pressing a gold coin into each outstretched, careworn hand. "Bless you!" cried the people.

A bird chirped loudly nearby—the bubble burst—the pretty scene dissolved. The baggy young man rubbed his forehead and frowned. "Oh no, you don't!"

he said severely to the house. "I don't even *want* to be that sort of a fellow. I'm here to be a tutor, remember, not a lord." And he picked up the old satchel firmly, opened the gate, and started up the path.

The beautiful house was set in equally beautiful, well-kept grounds. Off to the left, against a high hedge, a formal garden glowed moist and vibrant in the morning sun. Daffodils bloomed there now, and sturdy hyacinths, and a wide band of red tulips like a bright sash against the green of the hedge. Far to the right, at the edge of the lawn where a well-mannered wood began, stood a magnificent iron stag, its branching head tilted to listen and one slender foreleg lifted. The baggy young man paused and smiled. "Better run away!" he called to the stag. "Whoop! *Hey*—watch out! Hercules is here!" But the stag continued motionless, looking off over his head with its cool, indifferent iron eyes, and the baggy young man laughed and nodded to himself and went on up the path.

The next thing that happened happened so suddenly that it took a few moments to piece it together afterward. There he was walking calmly up the path when all at once there was a terrible crash of dishes from inside the house, the door burst open, and a small figure shot out, bounded down the steps, and ran right into him with a great bump that sent them both over backward. The satchel went spinning off into the grass and burst open like a ripe melon, a portion of its contents erupting onto the grass.

The baggy young man sat up and blinked, and the boy who had knocked him over sat up and blinked, too. They got to their feet, brushing gravel from the seats of their pants, and looked at each other warily.

"Who are *you?*" said the boy at last.

"I've come about the tutoring," said the baggy young man. "My name is Hercules Feltwright."

"Hercules?" said the boy. "Really? What kind of a name is that?"

"An unkind kind of name," said Hercules, "but I've learned to accept it. What's *your* name?"

"I'm Willet Goody," said the boy. "I live here. This is my house."

"Then it's you I've come to tutor," said Hercules Feltwright.

Willet Goody looked with interest at the long face

of the baggy young man. "How come you don't have any whiskers?" he asked. "Everyone has whiskers. My father's got yellow ones, a beard and everything."

"I like myself better this way," said Hercules. "Is your mother at home?"

"You'll see her in a minute, I expect," said Willet. "I just tripped old Dora and made her drop the breakfast tray, and she's gone to tell, the way she always does."

"Who's 'old Dora'?" asked Hercules.

"The housekeeper, Mrs. Tidings."

"Ah! The blacksmith's sister?"

"That's the one," said Willet. And then he pointed toward the gaping satchel. "What *is* all that?"

It was indeed a strange assortment lying about on the grass, but Hercules Feltwright was not apologetic as he went to repack. He called off the names of things as he put them back into the satchel. "Two embroidered vests. One cloak. Five pairs of tights. Hat. Box of paint. Another hat. False beard. Cat skin. Three under . . ."

"Wait!" Willet interrupted. "Wait! Can I see that cat skin? Where did you get that cat skin?"

"I'll tell you about it sometime," said Hercules. "Not now. Three undershirts. And—a book."

"What's the book?" asked Willet.

"Plays," said Hercules. "Shakespeare." And he closed up the satchel.

"Plays?"

"Yes."

"What for?"

"Pleasure."

"Oh," said Willet, seeming surprised. And then he said, "I don't like to read."

"That's too bad," said Hercules. "What *do* you like to do?"

"Well," said Willet, "if there was a dog around, I'd be pretty busy, but I'm not allowed to have one."

"That's a shame!" said Hercules. "Why not?"

"They scratch up the flower beds and shed hair all over the furniture," Willet explained. "So—I mostly just tease Mrs. Tidings."

"Hmm," said Hercules. "I thought perhaps it was an accident that you tripped the dear old soul."

"Bugfat," said Willet. "I meant to. And she's not

a dear old soul. She's big and her face is red and she's always watching."

Just then a soft voice called from the verandah. "Willet? Willet. Up here, please."

"That's my mother," said Willet. "Come on."

When Hercules Feltwright saw Mrs. Goody standing in the doorway of the beautiful house, he felt that there was something out of place. Here was the house, shining like a jewel box way out here in the country— the fact that it was there at all was surprising enough —and when the box was opened, it revealed, not a diamond necklace but a slice of bread. He would have had a hard time defending this impression, however, for Mrs. Goody was rather small and handsome and she wore a dressing gown drenched with lace. If you went by her appearance, she was not like a slice of bread at all, but rather a frosted muffin in a fluted paper cup. "But it was never the way she was dressed or anything like that," he always said afterward. "It was something about the anxious way she stood there, as if she were afraid someone was going to come and tell her she'd have to move along."

When he had climbed the steps and stood before her, he bowed and said, "Good morning. My name is Hercules Feltwright—I've come about the tutoring."

"He has a cat skin in his satchel, Mama," said Willet, coming up beside him. "I like him. Can he stay?"

Mrs. Goody frowned thoughtfully at Hercules. Her eyes were very blue and a little sad, he thought. "How do you do, I'm sure, Mr. Feltwright," she said. "How did you know I wanted a tutor? Well, never mind that. But you don't look like a tutor, do you? You don't look like . . . any profession in particular."

"I hope I only look like myself," said Hercules Feltwright.

Mrs. Goody's blue eyes narrowed. "Whatever do you mean," she asked, "by that remark?"

Hercules Feltwright stared. "Why, nothing!" he said hastily. "Nothing at all! That is, I *am* a teacher, truly I am, and I hope to be a good one."

"Very well," said Mrs. Goody, relaxing a little. "But—can you teach the proper things?"

"What things did you have in mind, ma'am?" asked Hercules with care.

Mrs. Goody looked taken aback. "Why, *you* know," she faltered. "The *proper* things. Whatever it is that tutors teach. I want Willet to be a gentleman. All children his age have tutors. That is," she added rather grandly, "all *wealthy* children."

"Oh," said Hercules. "Yes, I think I can teach him things like that."

Mrs. Goody turned to Willet. "Go in and eat your breakfast, Willet," she said. "And apologize to Mrs. Tidings. Do it nicely, mind you—she's very angry. You're a thoughtless, selfish boy to cause her so much trouble." But instead of frowning, Mrs. Goody's eyes went soft as she gazed at her son, and she smiled in spite of herself.

"I'm sorry, Mama," said Willet, and he smiled, too.

"Oh—and, Willet," said Mrs. Goody, "I have to go up to the city again this morning. I'll be gone the usual three or four days, I expect. I wish I didn't have to go, my love."

"Never mind, Mama," said Willet. "It's all right if Hercules is here." And he ran into the house.

Mrs. Goody turned back to the baggy young man. "He seems to have taken quite a shine to you," she said, giving him another long and thoughtful look. And then she seemed to make up her mind all at once. "I guess you'll do. Bring in your satchel and I'll ask Mrs. Tidings to show you to your room."

"Why, that's splendid," said Hercules Feltwright happily. "I'm very glad. This is my first tutoring position, but we'll get along, I'm sure, Willet and I. And it's such a beautiful house!"

At that, Mrs. Goody did something he was to remember for a long time afterward. She put out a hand and touched the shining brass knocker on the tall door, and she said with surprising fierceness, "Yes, it is. It *is* a beautiful house. It's everything in the world to me."

There was a moment of silence. "Hmm," said Hercules Feltwright to himself. Then he cleared his throat. "Excuse me," he said aloud, "but is Willet's father at home? Shouldn't I meet him too?"

Mrs. Goody's face changed. "Midas Goody is out there," she said abruptly, pointing across the lawn. "In the tomb beyond the hedge. He's dead."

"Dear me! I'm very sorry!" said Hercules.

"Don't mention it," said Mrs. Goody in a cold voice.

"Don't mention it ever again. He's dead and that's all there is to it." Then she gathered the skirts of her dressing gown around her, and her first, softer voice returned. "Go and get your satchel, Mr. Feltwright," she said. "I'm glad you've come." And she turned and disappeared inside the beautiful house.

CHAPTER 3

It's important to understand that Hercules Feltwright did not believe he was a hero like the mythological Hercules for whom he was named. Heroes are larger than life, and muscular, and brave as lions—or so we like to picture them—while Hercules Feltwright was tall and thin and rather stringy, and his courage was not at all the lion kind. However, Hercules Feltwright, son of a hatter and descendant of a long line of hatters, had been reminded time and time again of certain similarities between things that happened to him and things that had happened to the first Hercules in all the old stories. Only coincidences, to be sure, but Hercules Feltwright resented them just the same because he didn't want to be like the first Hercules, in spite of the fact that his mother had given him the name with that very hope in her heart —a hero for a son!—as if the name alone could make it come true. And he didn't want to be a hatter, either, when it came to that, in spite of the fact that his father had that very hope in *his* heart—a hatter for a son!— as if birth into the family automatically gave him a passion for the trade.

Hercules Feltwright wished instead to be his own true self, which is the best wish of all. But as long as he stayed at home, it was a difficult wish to realize. He was trained, of course, to be a hatter. His father trained him. And as luck would have it, he turned out to be rather good at it. His father was not surprised. After all, wasn't the boy a Feltwright? But Hercules was surprised, and more than a little discouraged. And then, in addition, there were the things that kept happening to him which his mother insisted on comparing to the things that had happened to the first Hercules.

For instance, when he was a baby a neighbor's child put an earthworm into his cradle and he rolled over on it in his sleep and mashed it flat. His mother was overjoyed. Hadn't the first Hercules killed a crawling thing in *his* cradle when *he* was only a baby? Yes, but in the case of the first Hercules the crawling thing was a large poisonous snake and the infant strangled it with his bare hands! Never mind that. There may have been small differences here and there, but it was still the same thing in general, she reasoned; and it was a sign—a hero for a son!—a very promising sign.

There were other coincidences. There was the time when a neighborhood cat named Neemie went mad. Hercules, then a boy of eight, caught it and killed it after it had terrorized the village for a week. There! Didn't that prove it again? Here was the first Hercules once more, gone out to capture the ferocious Nemean Lion for the first of his Twelve Labors. Wasn't a lion nothing but a cat when you came right down to it? Why, the names were the same, even, or almost, anyway. Mrs. Feltwright was ecstatic. She insisted that her son keep the cat's skin for a trophy. It wasn't nearly large enough to wear, as the first Hercules had worn his lion's skin, but it was a symbol just the same.

And then, most recently, there was the time when Mrs. Feltwright sent her son to a farm in the country to buy a sackful of those good big yellow apples. And all the time she kept remembering how the first Hercules was sent, for his eleventh Labor, to fetch the Golden Apples of the Hesperides. When Hercules Feltwright returned with a bulging sack, he mentioned that on the way he had come across a man tied up in a cornfield like a scarecrow, with a lot of irritating crows perching on his shoulders. He had chased the crows away and set the man free. Turning pale, his mother begged for details. Well, it seemed that the fellow was a tutor to a rich man's children and was being punished for teaching them how to build a fire. At this, Mrs. Feltwright fainted dead away and, when revived, could talk of nothing else for days but the story of Prometheus and how the first Hercules had set *him* free from the rock to which he had been chained for bringing the secret of fire to mortals. An interesting comparison, no use denying that, but nothing more than a comparison, and the end of it was that Hercules Feltwright grew very weary. He left home at the age of seventeen and he went out into the world to find his own way, whatever that might turn out to be.

His father was sure that Hercules would come to his senses and return to hats and home someday, so he wasn't too upset. But Mrs. Feltwright was very disappointed because she knew what the last of the Twelve Labors held in store: a descent to the Gates of Hell, nothing less, and a dangerous encounter with the terrible three-headed dog, Cerberus, who stood guard there. She was utterly convinced that some form of this horror awaited her son and she wanted to be there when he emerged triumphant, in order to make comparisons.

But it was not to be: Hercules Feltwright had gone away and was loose in the world, traveling about with a troupe of touring players, for he had decided that the practical way to accomplish his ends was to become an actor. "That way," he reasoned, "I can try on as many different selves as possible and choose the one that seems to be the best and most comfortable fit." And this is exactly how it worked out. He ranged far and wide with the troupe for a number of years, acting first in one role and then in another, and at last, after a long tour as a wise old schoolmaster in one of the plays, he was able to decide, with the simple joy that all right decisions bring, that the only and perfect thing for him to be was a teacher. "*Here*" (he had quoted, or rather misquoted, from the play)

> "*Shall I, shy schoolmaster, make me more prophet*
> *Than ever princes can, and have more time*
> *For saner hours, and tutor what I care for.*"

And so, with a new kind of confidence, he left the troupe of actors and wandered off, a tall, stringy, baggy young man wearing the rather peculiar clothes he had come to feel at home in, and beardless in an age of beards because he liked it that way; and he came at last, at the ripe old age of twenty-five, to Goody Hall.

CHAPTER 4

Mrs. Goody went away to the city in the middle of the morning, and within minutes, as so often happens when the head of the house goes off, the atmosphere at Goody Hall relaxed a little. But only a little. The house itself commanded a certain formality, and Mrs. Tidings seemed determined to see that no one lost sight of the fact. Serving the meal at lunchtime, she tramped in and out of the elegant dining room with its filmy cloth and sparkling chandelier, and she was like nothing so much as an understudy who is finally getting a chance to take over the starring role. Or at least that is what Hercules Feltwright thought as he watched her. And she, of course, watched him and had her own thoughts, none of them good if you went by her expression. However, she spoke only to Willet, who slumped in lonely magnificence at one end of the shining table while Hercules had to make do halfway down one side.

Not that he would have called it "making do," however, for he was quite overcome by his surroundings, though Mrs. Tidings didn't seem to notice this. She placed things in front of him without comment, and after a while he relaxed a little and was able to eat without being afraid he would swallow crooked and disgrace himself by choking to death.

"Your mother's gone off to the city again, I see, Master Willet," Mrs. Tidings observed in an encouraging tone as she brought around the soup.

"Yes," said Willet, testing his bowlful and pushing it away. (Hercules, on the other hand, tried his and, like Goldilocks, found it just right and ate it all up.)

"She visits all the fancy shops, I suppose," said Mrs. Tidings idly on her next trip round with a platter of fish.

"Yes," said Willet, "I suppose she does."

Beets and boiled potatoes came next and with these Mrs. Tidings offered another pointed observation: "She never buys anything in those fancy shops, though."

But Willet only said, "No, I guess not," and Mrs. Tidings, muttering something about clams, was forced to retire to the kitchen.

She made the most of her last appearance. She came in bearing the pudding like a bribe and spooned out a large helping for Willet, which she then anointed with cream and held up just out of his reach. "I can't understand why a person would go all the way to the city twice a year and always come back empty-handed," she said, looking fondly at the pudding.

"It's strange, all right," said Willet. "I'll have that pudding now." And of course she had to give it to him.

Afterward, Willet and Hercules went outside and sat on the lawn beside the iron stag, where the afternoon sun, slanting down through the leaves of the well-mannered wood, strewed everything with golden blobs of trembling light. Across the grass, on the other side of the house where the garden lay, an old man in shabby clothes knelt with a basket at his side, pulling weeds slowly and carefully. From his trouser pocket a bright red handkerchief dangled like a warning flag and from time to time he would haul it out and mop at the back of his neck.

"That's the gardener," Willet explained. "His name is Alfresco Rom. And he's got a daughter named Alfreida. Hey there, Alfresco!" he called. "How are the weeds today?"

The old man turned his head and looked at them. His wrinkled face, burned brown by the sun and furnished with a large, shaggy moustache, was set in a sour and permanent frown which as much as said that, no matter what you were doing, you were a lazy good-for-nothing and he wished you would leave him alone. He scowled at them for a moment without speaking and then he tossed his tools into his basket, stood up, and stalked off out of sight behind the house.

"You must have made him angry!" said Hercules.

"Never mind," said Willet. "He's always like that, no matter what you say to him. I like him, though. He gives me worms sometimes."

"Oh!" said Hercules. "That's all right then. But you'd think it would be hard to be cross on a day like this." He sighed contentedly and stretched out on his back in the grass with his eyes closed. A circle of sunlight wobbled on his cheek and a passing bee paused hopefully for an instant above his nose—was this some strange new variety of flower?—and then, seeing its mistake, buzzed away in disgust.

Willet Goody chewed on a blade of grass and watched his new tutor with interest. "That bee was going to sting you," he remarked.

"Oh, I don't think so," said Hercules comfortably. He began to hum under his breath, waving one hand lazily, and then the hum opened up into the song he had been singing earlier on the road:

"*Where the sea bucks, there buck I.*
In a proud ship's bell I lie.
Dum da de dum, de dum dum,
Dum da dum, I forget this part,
Mariner, mariner shall I live now,
Under the mosses that hang on the prow."

"That's a silly song," said Willet when it was over. "It doesn't make any sense!"

"Certainly it makes sense," Hercules objected. "I learned it in a play. A wonderful play about a shipwreck."

"Oh!" said Willet. "You were in a play once?"

"Once and then some," said Hercules. "I was an actor for a long while. Traveled all over with a troupe of touring players." He sat up and leaned his elbows on his knees. "They let me take all kinds of parts. Princes, fools, wise old men. I enjoyed it very much."

"Do some!" Willet commanded. "Do a prince!"

Hercules scratched his head. "Well, let's see now. I always did have trouble remembering lines, but I think I could piece together one prince part. It goes something like this." He stood up and, laying a hand on his heart, threw back his head and bellowed:

> *"O! that this cuckoo's stolid vest would moult,*
> *Yaw, and revolve itself into a smew!*
> *Or that the ever-laughing had not set*
> *His gannet 'gainst well water.*
> *Fie on't! O fie! 'tis an unguarded weed*
> *That sows to greed; things lank in nomenclature*
> *Profess it clearly."*

On the side of the house facing them, a window flew open and Mrs. Tidings poked her head out. "Let up on the racket, for the Lord's sake," she cried. "Can't hear myself think in here." Then the window slammed shut again.

"Your housekeeper doesn't seem to care for poetry," said Hercules, sitting down with a bump.

"I guess not," said Willet, giggling. And then he added in a disgusted tone, "She's always trying to get me to tell her things about my mother."

"I noticed that at lunch," said Hercules. "What does she do that for?"

Willet looked at him and then looked away quickly. "I don't know," he said, and changed the subject adroitly. "I wish you'd tell me about that cat skin."

"What cat skin?"

"Why, the one in your satchel. The one I saw this morning."

"Oh," said Hercules. "I was afraid that was the one you meant. Well. It's not easy to explain. And it sounds a little silly."

"That's all right," said Willet. "I still want to hear about it."

"Well," said Hercules again. He rubbed his nose, and when he began to speak, his explanation came in one long, hurried sentence. "You see, my mother thought that maybe I was the old Greek hero Hercules born again and one day I had to kill a cat because it had gone crazy and was scaring people and she decided it was just like Hercules killing a lion and wearing the skin and she thought the cat skin was a good-luck souvenir and she wanted me to keep it." He stopped and took a deep breath, clearly embarrassed.

"You don't look anything like the real Hercules,"

said Willet critically. "He had a whole lot of muscles."

"I know it," said Hercules Feltwright apologetically, "but my mother had this idea and she couldn't give it up. Although," he paused reflectively, "she almost did one time when Mott Snave stole the statue of Cerberus. That was quite a disappointment for her."

"Oh!" said Willet, leaning forward eagerly. "Do you know the stories about Mott Snave? He wasn't real, though. He's a legend, like Robbing Hood."

"He was, too, real!" protested Hercules. "And it isn't Robbing Hood, it's *Robin* Hood."

"Listen," said Willet. "I ought to know about Mott Snave, I guess. Alfreida, she's the gardener's daughter, she's been telling me stories about him for ages, whenever she's got time to sit down. And she says it's only a legend. They're secret stories, too. I'm not supposed to repeat them to anyone, not even my mother. But that's all right. I like secrets."

"Well, there's nothing secret about Mott Snave where *I* come from," said Hercules. "And he was just as real as you or I. But there's no point in arguing about it. What did Alfreida tell you about him?"

"There are a whole lot of stories," said Willet. "Mostly about how he used to steal things and hide them, and no matter where he hid them, a man named John Constant would find them and give them back to the people he'd stolen them from."

"That's right," said Hercules. "John Constant was a farmer who lived up there and he did always find the stolen things."

"Well, that proves it," said Willet. "That wouldn't really happen."

"I admit it's peculiar," said Hercules. "But it did happen."

"Bugfat," snorted Willet. "Anyway, then Mott Snave stole a big silver statue of Cerberus."

"Yes, he did," said Hercules. "The three-headed dog! My mother was so disappointed. She always hoped I'd get involved with that statue because she was—well, she was always looking for coincidences, and when she couldn't find any, she sometimes set them up herself."

"But what has that got to do with Cerberus?" asked Willet.

"Why," said his tutor, "Cerberus was the dog who guarded the Gates of Hell in all the old stories. The first Hercules was sent down to bring him up, and he did it, too, but then he took him back again."

"Well," said Willet, "in Alfreida's story Mott Snave sneaked into the house of the bishop who owned the statue and stole it right out from under his nose, and the bishop chased him and fell into a well and drowned." He giggled.

"You shouldn't laugh about it, Willet," said Hercules. "It was a very sad thing."

"But it didn't really happen!" said Willet. "And even if it was true, I still think it's kind of funny."

"Well, a silver statue of Cerberus was a funny thing for a bishop to own, there's no doubt about that," said Hercules. "He bragged about it from one end of the county to the other. Anyone who could steal it could keep it, he used to say. An open invitation to a thief if I ever heard one. And who'd want it anyway? It must have been an ugly old thing. But Snave wanted it, for some reason or other, and he got it, too. And disappeared forever."

"I know why he wanted it," said Willet. "That's

another one of the stories. Alfreida says it was full of jewels and Mott Snave stole it away and took the jewels and built a castle and married Cinderella and lived unhappily ever after."

"Unhappily?"

"That's what Alfreida says."

"Well, I never heard anything about any jewels," said Hercules. "She made that part up."

"But it's *all* made up, Hercules," Willet insisted. "After all, did you ever *see* Mott Snave?"

"No, of course not! It all happened when I was a little boy. My mother told me about it when I got older."

"She was just repeating a legend, then. Like Robbing Hood."

"*Robin* Hood, for goodness' sake!" said Hercules. "And it isn't a legend, I tell you. It's all true. John Constant was a real farmer who really found the things Snave stole. He disappeared himself, too, by the way, not long after. And the bishop was real—it's all true. Except for the part about the statue being full of jewels, and the castle and Cinderella."

"Bugfat," said Willet again. "Your mother was

just fooling you. None of it is true." And then he added, suddenly serious, "*My* mother can't fool *me*, though."

Mott Snave was forgotten at once. Hercules looked at the boy curiously. "But, Willet!" he said. "Why should your mother want to fool you?"

Willet shrugged his shoulders. "I don't know. But she does. I guess she has a reason, but I don't know what it is." He stopped and looked hard and long at Hercules. "Can you keep a secret?" he asked at last. "A secret I've never told to anyone in the whole world?"

"Certainly," said Hercules.

"Well then," said Willet, "come on. I'll show you something." He got up and ran across the grass to the other side of the lawn, skirted around the formal garden, and paused at the hedge. When Hercules caught up with him, he squeezed himself through a thin place in the scratchy branches and motioned Hercules to follow.

On the other side of the hedge, ringed by a circle of poplars, stood a small square building made of stone. In a slab above the stout wooden door, the carved words *Midas Goody* announced the building's purpose beyond mistake.

"That's my father's tomb," said Willet. "You go inside that door and you go down some steps and the coffin's down there. I made Alfresco tell me all about it."

"Good grief, Willet!" said Hercules in pained surprise.

"That's all right," said Willet with a little smile. "You see, the coffin's down there, all right, but my father isn't in it. And the reason he isn't in it is because he isn't dead."

Hercules looked at the boy for a long moment and at last he said, "Not dead?"

"Don't look so solemn, Hercules," said Willet. "There's nothing to be solemn about. The reason I know he isn't dead is because my mother was never even sad. She told me he fell off his horse and was killed, but she wasn't sad, she was cross. And she was cross for weeks afterward."

"She wasn't sad?" said Hercules.

"No, she wasn't. The horse never came back, either. And Hercules, there's one more thing. I was hiding in the hedge when they carried the coffin down the steps into the tomb. They thought I was in the house, but I was really in the hedge. The coffin bumped against the wall and something inside it went *clank*."

"Clank?" said Hercules.

"Clank," said Willet.

They stood side by side staring at the tomb.

"My father wouldn't have gone *clank*," observed Willet calmly, "so he isn't in the coffin. And if he isn't in the coffin, he isn't dead."

"Then," wondered Hercules, feeling more like the taught than the tutor, "where is he?"

"I don't know," said Willet. And then he added, in a voice full of patient confidence, "But he'll come back someday. Just wait and see."

"Not dead?" said Hercules.

"No," said Willet.

A lengthening afternoon shadow fell across the face of the tomb, and the letters *Midas Goody* disappeared.

CHAPTER 5

At supper there was no sign of Mrs. Tidings, although they could hear her perfectly well stomping about in the kitchen to the music of clattering pots and dishes. Instead, the meal was served by someone entirely new to Hercules—a rather short, round young woman with chopped-off black hair who was probably, he supposed, Alfreida Rom, the gardener's daughter, who told all the Mott Snave stories to Willet. She turned on Hercules one sharp, search-ing glance which seemed to stab right into his soul and immediately he felt nervous and unworthy. He wanted to kneel down and swear to be a better man by morning, but instead he sat and clutched his napkin.

Willet, however, looked at her with obvious pleas-ure. "Hullo, Alfreida!" he said. "Where were you all day?"

"Never mind, dearie," she replied, slapping down a bowl of soup in front of him. "Where I go is none of your affair. Who's the do-nothing with the bare face?" And she pointed at Hercules as if he were a picture on the wall.

"That's my new tutor," said Willet. "His name is Hercules Feltwright."

Alfreida looked at Hercules with an expression very like disgust, and Willet, following her example, looked at him, too. There was a long moment of silence during which Hercules, under their combined gaze, grew even more nervous and dropped a spoon.

"So you're a tutor, are you, dearie?" Alfreida said at last, after he had fished the spoon out from under his chair and sat up again, red-faced and breathless.

"That's right!" said Hercules heartily, and felt at once that his voice was too loud and that Alfreida would despise him for it.

"He used to be an actor once," said Willet, attacking the soup. "He's got a cat skin and a false beard."

"Well now! Is that right!" said Alfreida, softening a little. Suddenly she smiled, revealing a gold tooth. "He might be all right then, after all," she nodded to Willet. "An actor, eh? I was afraid he'd be one of these walking books you see around sometimes. *You* know—hands behind the back, thin legs; but an actor . . . that's not so bad." She pulled out a chair opposite Hercules and sat down, leaning her elbows on the table. "I've got two careers myself," she said to him. "Helping out at Goody Hall isn't all I do."

"No?" said Hercules, greatly relieved that she had decided to accept him. "What else?"

Alfreida lowered her voice. "I'm a medium, dearie. If you ever want to call someone back from the dead, just come to me. Any evening—we have a little house, my father and me, just this side of the village."

"That's . . . uh . . . very kind of you," said

Hercules, feeling a little nervous again. "A medium, eh? Well, well. I was in a play once that had three witches. How did that go now? Oh, yes, I remember:

*"Rumble, rumble, foil and fumble,
    Choir adjourn and children mumble."*

Alfreida made a face. "Witches!" she snorted. "That's for amateurs." She stood up and replaced the chair with an imperious shove. "What I do is the real thing, not a lot of mumbo-jumbo. Prince Albert himself comes when *I* call."

At that moment a sharp voice barked from the kitchen. "Alfreida? Bring out those soup plates and stop all the yammering." And then the voice, somewhat lower but clearly intending to be heard, added: "Some people don't know their place and never will."

Alfreida smiled again and the gold tooth winked. "Any time at all, dearie," she said to Hercules in a loud whisper. "It doesn't matter whether they've been dead two years or a hundred. They all come flapping when it's me who wants them." Then she picked up the soup plates, taking her time about it, and disappeared into the kitchen.

"My goodness!" said Hercules, staring after her.

Willet beamed. "That's the one good thing when my mother goes away! Alfreida never talks any other time. She must like you, or she'd never have said a word."

The rest of the dinner went peacefully enough, and afterward things grew very quiet at Goody Hall. Alfreida went home to fix her father's supper ("Bat wings and toad legs, I suppose," said Hercules, not without admiration) and Mrs. Tidings retired with her mending to her own room, after speaking severely to Hercules.

"Willet is your responsibility now. See that he gets to bed on time. And he's not to be upset by too much excitement—a story or some quiet conversation at the most—those are Mrs. Goody's orders. She dotes on that boy, and if you know what's good for you, you'll see he's made happy and comfortable."

Hercules was indignant. "It wouldn't occur to me to do anything else!" he protested.

"I just thought I'd tell you," Mrs. Tidings said in a superior tone. "And remember—I'll be watching."

"She will, too," said Willet sadly after she had gone. "She can see right through the walls."

"Well, she can't see up to my room," said Hercules. "Come on up and I'll show you that cat skin before bedtime."

The room that had been assigned to Hercules was on the second floor of the beautiful house, and it was right next to Willet's. There was even a door between, which made it all quite cozy and friendly. Willet's room was much larger, of course, and had an elegant marble fireplace, while Hercules had only brick, but still it was the nicest room he'd ever occupied. In fact, it was so nice that he wondered whether he'd ever be able to go to sleep in it—and then he noticed that outside an enormous lilac bush was in full bloom, and when he opened his window a lush branch that had been pressing against the glass came bobbing in with its shiny heart-shaped leaves, and the heavy purple clusters filled the room with their sweet scent. "Lilacs!" he exclaimed. "My very favorite flower! I'd rather have lilacs than all the perfumes of Arabia."

"Where's the cat skin?" asked Willet.

"The darling buds of May!" breathed Hercules, still at the window.

"Hercules!" said Willet impatiently. "Come on and show me the cat skin."

"Oh yes. All right. The cat skin." Hercules turned away from the lilacs and crossed the room to the big dark-wood wardrobe. He swung its double doors wide. Inside, Mrs. Tidings had hung all his interesting clothes properly on hangers, and sure enough, shoved way over to one side by itself, the cat skin was draped on a hanger of its own. "There it is," said Hercules, taking it down and handing it to Willet. "It's not in very good condition, I'm afraid. I've had it for seventeen years."

Willet took the limp skin reverently and rubbed its meager fur against his cheek. "It's beautiful!" he sighed. "I wish I had one."

"Well, I'll tell you what," said Hercules. "I'll give it to you. I should have gotten rid of it long ago. It was a silly idea to begin with."

"Do you really mean it, Hercules?"

"Of course I mean it. It's yours," said his tutor.

"It's the best thing I ever had in all my life," said Willet with conviction. He carried the skin happily to his own room and in a moment he was back. "What else have you got that's interesting?"

"Well, let's see," said Hercules. "How about nose putty? Ever see any up close? They use it all the time in plays."

"I've never been to a play," said Willet, sitting down on the bed and looking at Hercules expectantly.

"What? Never been to a play? I can hardly believe it." He crossed to the bureau and began pulling drawers open. "Where's my box? My make-up box? I'm not used to someone else putting away all my . . . oh, here it is." He took it out of the bottom drawer, opened it, and fished out a lump of pinkish, clay-like stuff which he squeezed with his fingers for a few moments until it was soft. Then he clapped it over his nose.

Willet burst out laughing. "You look so funny— like a whole other person!"

Hercules went to the long mirror that stood in the corner and peered at himself. "Not bad," he said. He fussed with the putty, molding it into a somewhat more reasonable shape. "Yes, you can change yourself altogether with a bit of this stuff." He turned his head from side to side, admiring the large new nose, and then he paused. "All I need now is . . ."

Shrugging out of his baggy jacket, he went to the wardrobe and began to pull things out and put them on. A dark vest. A black cloak. A flat black hat with an obscuring brim. And a long red scarf which he wound around his neck and up over his mouth until only the nose poked out over it. Then he returned to the mirror. "There!" His voice came muffled through the folds of the scarf. "Now—who am I?" He turned around and faced Willet, slinking a few steps forward and narrowing his eyes under the shadowy hat brim.

"Mott Snave!" cried Willet, utterly delighted.

"Right! I'm Mott Snave, the jewel thief!" the muffled voice growled. "Hand over the diamond necklace!"

"Oh, Hercules!" crowed Willet. "It's just wonderful. That's exactly how Alfreida described him."

Hercules turned back to the mirror. "Yes," he said in his normal voice, "this was the sort of costume he wore. Black hat, cloak, red scarf. A pretty picture on a dark night. It's interesting, though," he added, giving the tip of the putty nose another squeeze. "I wonder how Alfreida knew about him."

"Oh, Alfreida's a gypsy," said Willet. "Gypsies always know everything. And they love to tell stories. Mrs. Tidings said so."

"That's nonsense," said Hercules. "Alfreida isn't a gypsy. Gypsies don't settle down in villages and do housework; they stick together and travel around."

"Well," said Willet, "she certainly looks like a gypsy. Mrs. Tidings says she does, anyway."

"Mrs. Tidings says a lot of things," observed his tutor.

"Hercules!" said Willet, suddenly struck with an idea. "Hercules, listen! Go down and knock on the door and see if you can fool her!"

"Fool Mrs. Tidings? Oh, I'd better not do that," said Hercules, shaking his head inside the scarf. "Dressing up is only for plays. And anyway, she might be frightened."

"Nothing frightens *her*," said Willet. "Come on, Hercules! Just to see if she can tell who you are. We can pretend it's a play, can't we?"

Hercules turned and, looking over the putty nose at Willet's eager face, was touched by the pleasure he saw there. "Well," he said, relenting, "I don't suppose it would really do any harm. All right. If you're sure it won't alarm her. You can watch from the top of the stairs."

Together they crept out of the room and peered over the railing into the shadowy hall below, where the blue twilight made everything look new and mysterious. "There's the stage down there," whispered Hercules, "and here's your seat in the balcony. Sit down and be very quiet. The play is about to begin."

He started softly down the staircase, the cloak whispering about his ankles. When he reached the bottom, he turned and looked back up to where Willet crouched in the darkness on the top step. Then he pulled the scarf higher under the putty nose and flung back his shoulders. Suddenly, and remarkably, he was no longer a baggy young man named Hercules Feltwright; instead he was cold, shrewd, fearless—he was Mott Snave, master thief. With the greatest care, he opened the tall front door. For a moment the dry song of crickets seemed to roar into the hall and then with a swish of cloak he was through the door and had closed it behind him. Willet waited, breathless, and almost at once came a series of loud, commanding raps. Then Mrs. Tidings was thumping down the hall, holding a lighted candle. She arrived below him, immense in a flowered wrapper, and flung open the door.

"Well, who is it?" she barked. "What do you mean by waking people up in the middle of the night?"

Mott Snave stood there like a shadow. The evening breeze stirred the folds of his cloak and in the twilight the red scarf looked purple. The putty nose gleamed faintly. When he spoke, his voice was deep and slow through the scarf. "I understand there's a young man here—a certain Hercules Feltwright," he said. "Is that correct?"

"That's correct," said Mrs. Tidings without the least alarm. "What do you want with him?"

"He's a friend of mine," answered the voice. "Can you tell me—did he bring Cerberus with him?"

Mrs. Tidings made an annoyed exclamation. "I'm not going to tell you anything," she said crossly. "If you want to see him, you'll have to wait until tomor-

row. This is no hour of the night for curious visitors.
Get along now and don't come back till morning."
She shut the door firmly and went back down the hall
with her candle, muttering to herself. "A fine thing
. . . wrapped up like a mummy on a night like this
. . . some people . . . never a thought for others."
Then her bedroom door closed and there was silence.
At the top of the stairs Willet uncurled himself and
stood up gleefully. Hercules had fooled her com-
pletely.

The front door opened and shut once more, and
Mott Snave hurried up the stairs, turning back into
Hercules as he came. In the bedroom, unwinding the
scarf, he said, "Well, you were right! She wasn't
frightened at all, thank goodness. I must say *I* enjoyed
it. Makes me miss the old days."

"It was just fine," said Willet. "Is that what a real
play is like?"

"Well, more or less," said Hercules, peeling off
the putty nose. "Except, in a real play, of course, Mrs.
Tidings would have known it was only me, and she
wouldn't have been playing herself, you know. She'd
have been acting the part of—oh, the giant's wife,

perhaps, or maybe grandmother of the wind." He stood looking at himself critically in the mirror. "That was a very good nose," he said. "Much more interesting than mine. Big noses have such a lot of strength and character."

"It looked like my father's nose," said Willet, picking up the putty and squeezing it.

"Really? Your father had a big nose?" And then, "I mean—*has* a big nose?"

"Yes, he does," said Willet. "I haven't seen him for a long time, but I remember his face exactly." He yawned.

"It's way past your bedtime," said Hercules, suddenly collecting himself. "Go to bed, Willet. That's all the dressing up we're going to do. I'm here to be a tutor, not an actor."

"But it was fun, wasn't it?" said Willet happily. "What are you going to tell Mrs. Tidings in the morning? You'd better not tell her it was you at the door—she'll be awfully cross."

"For goodness' sake—I never even thought of that!" said Hercules in dismay. "You're right, of course. She'll be angry and she'll tell your mother and then I won't be your tutor any more." He scratched his head thoughtfully. "I should have listened to my own advice. Dressing up is only for plays. Well, it looks as if this play will have to go into a second act. I'll have to make up something and hope it will satisfy her."

"What will you say?" asked Willet with interest.

"I really don't know! This is what happens when you start out to . . . Well, you remember the old saw: 'Oh, what a mangled web we . . . uh . . . leave . . .' "

"Not that way," said Willet. "It goes: 'Oh, what a tangled web we weave, when first we practice to deceive.' But don't worry, Hercules, it's only for fun." And then, in that suddenly adult way he had that seemed so sad and so surprising, he added, "This house is already full of tangled webs anyway. Someday I'm going to untangle every one, and then maybe my father will come home again."

"I hope so," said Hercules gently. "Good night."

"Good night," said Willet.

CHAPTER 6

Breakfast at Goody Hall turned out to be just as formal a meal as lunch and supper. And if the morning hadn't been so deliciously sweet and sunny, Hercules Feltwright might have been a little discouraged. He came down to the table dressed for his first full day of tutorhood in the usual baggy trousers, but from the waist up he was decidedly unusual. There was a rather loose shirt striped in particularly tender shades of lavender, and over this a long vest heavily embroidered with rose-like splotches and little yellow dragons with their tails in their mouths. At least, they appeared to be dragons, but might just as well have been bananas or even sheaves of wheat. Hercules was particularly proud of this shirt and vest—he had worn them in a play—and he had decided that they struck just the right note for a casual breakfast in the country.

Mrs. Tidings didn't agree. She came into the dining room carrying a large bowl of stewed prunes and she stopped dead when she saw him. "What in the world is that?" she said in a shocked kind of way.

"What is what?" asked Hercules, taking his place at the table and beaming a cheery good-morning smile at Willet.

"You can't come into the dining room dressed like that," said Mrs. Tidings. "Not in *this* house."

"Why not?" asked Hercules in hurt surprise. "What's the matter with the way I'm dressed?"

"Come come, Mr. Feltwright," she chided. "Look around you. Surely even you can see it isn't proper."

Hercules looked around obediently, and the dining

room frowned back at him. The lace curtains shivered slightly, the sideboard gleamed heavy disapproval, and from the mantelpiece over the graceful white fireplace a pair of smirking gilded cupids stared at him reproachfully. Hercules stared back at the cupids. Then he looked at Willet, and Willet was looking back at him, waiting. At last Hercules Feltwright shook a defiant mental fist under the nose of the beautiful house and picked up his napkin. "Pride goeth before, if at all," he said with a meaningful smile. But there was no meaning at all in what he had said, no meaning that Mrs. Tidings could discover, and she was just about to point this out when Willet interrupted.

"I like the way he's dressed," he said. "I think it's beautiful."

Mrs. Tidings gave it up. This, after all, was the word of the master. Let no one ever think she didn't know her place. But her expression clearly said, "We'll see about that when Mrs. Goody comes home!" She dished out the prunes and turned toward the kitchen. And then she stopped and turned back to

Hercules. "By the way, Mr. Feltwright," she said, with the smug look of someone who has found a way to have the last word, "I think you should tell your friends not to come calling in the middle of the night."

Hercules made a little face at Willet which seemed to say "Here we go!" "What friends?" he asked innocently, spooning up a prune.

Mrs. Tidings looked at him closely. "Well!" she said. "You had a caller last night. He wanted to know if you were here and he asked me if you had Sir Bursus with you."

Willet giggled and Hercules sent him a warning glance. "What did he look like?" he asked.

"He was all wrapped up in a cloak and a heavy scarf," said Mrs. Tidings.

Hercules returned a prune to his bowl and stared at her in mock alarm. "A *red* scarf?" he asked.

"I really couldn't say," said Mrs. Tidings. "Why?"

"If it was a red scarf," said Hercules, "it must have been . . . no, it couldn't have . . . yes, it must have been Mott Snave."

"Well," said Mrs. Tidings, "you'll have to tell him

we don't receive callers at Goody Hall after four o'clock in the afternoon." She looked at Hercules suspiciously. "Who's Sir Bursus?"

"Not Sir Bursus. *Cerberus*."

"All right, then, who's Cerberus?"

"Why, the three-headed dog at the Gates of Hell, of course."

Mrs. Tidings frowned impatiently. "What kind of nonsense is that?" she said.

"Oh, not the very dog himself, of course. A statue of him. A big silver statue."

"Have you got it?"

"The statue, you mean? No, *I* haven't got it. I've never even heard of it."

"What do you mean, you've never even heard of it?" she barked. "You've just been telling me all about it!"

"Not *all* about it, by any means," said Hercules in a wise and careful tone. "And anyway," he added, victim of a sudden and rather unfortunate inspiration which later he always blamed on the influence of the beautiful house, "perhaps it isn't really Cerberus

Snave is after. Perhaps he's found out about my inheritance."

Mrs. Tidings opened her mouth to retort and then she paused. Her face changed, as if she'd just been told she was on the brink of throwing away an oyster which contained a pearl. "Your . . . inheritance?" she echoed.

"Oh well," said Hercules, looking modest, "I have an old aunt who's putting a few pennies aside for me."

Mrs. Tidings put down the serving bowl of prunes and smoothed her apron reflectively. She thought about this aunt. The dear old creature! It just went to show, you should never judge a man too quickly. "Well now, Mr. Feltwright, isn't that nice?" she said warmly. "Where does your aunt live? Far from here? Are you the only relative? Why don't you invite her in for tea? And Snave, too, or whatever his name is."

Hercules saw at last that he had gone too far. Willet, at the head of the table, saw it, too, and grinned through a mouthful of prunes.

"Now see here, Mrs. Tidings," said Hercules

hastily. "Never mind about my aunt. She lives a long way from here. And if Snave comes back, you can tell him I don't want to see him. He's not a friend of mine at all. I've never even met him." And he began to eat prunes with remarkable speed.

Mrs. Tidings smiled knowingly. "Very well, sir," she said. "I understand. I'll see you're not troubled any further. There's always someone around who wants to borrow money, isn't there? It must be quite a burden." And she picked up the serving bowl and disappeared into the kitchen.

After breakfast, Hercules and Willet escaped and rushed outside to sit beside the iron stag. "Good grief!" said Hercules, shaking his head. "What on earth made me go and say all that? Now she thinks I'm rich."

"Well, you as good as told her you were," said Willet gleefully. "Do you really have an old aunt who's going to leave you some money?"

"Yes, I do!" said Hercules. "I told the exact truth. She's doing just what I said she was doing—putting a few pennies aside for me. Pennies with holes in them, bent pennies, pennies with the printing crooked. I used to collect them when I was a boy, and she's still saving them for me. At least, she was when I left home eight years ago." He sighed. "I guess I've only made things worse, haven't I?"

Willet chewed a blade of grass. "You could always dress up as Mott Snave again and come back and tell Mrs. Tidings something else. You know—tell her about the penny collection and maybe give her a bent penny to give to you. I mean, give to Hercules. As a present from your aunt, you know. Or something like that."

"Yes, I suppose I could do that," said Hercules. "That might work. But I certainly do hate to go on to Act Three. We never even should have raised the curtain." He stared off across the lawn and sighed again. "Well, this isn't getting any lessons done, is it? And that's what I'm here for."

Now it was Willet's turn to sigh. "Do we have to?" he said.

"Yes," said Hercules, "we have to. Your mother

wants you to grow up to be a gentleman, like your father. Now, what shall we begin with? Poetry? Or perhaps posture and manners? Or else . . ."

"Hercules," Willet interrupted suddenly. "Why do you suppose my father wanted to go away? I just can't figure it out."

Hercules decided, looking at Willet, that perhaps the lessons should be put aside for a little longer. "What do you remember about your father?" he asked.

Willet gave his tutor a grateful glance. "I was only five years old when he went away," he said. "I don't remember much. He built this house for my mother when I was a baby. I don't remember *that*, of course. But when I was bigger, he used to play with me all the time. But sometimes he wasn't very happy —I do remember that, I think. And when he was unhappy, he would go rushing away on a big horse. And then one morning my mother told me he'd fallen off the horse and he was dead. But I knew it wasn't true."

Hercules was quiet until Willet had finished and then he said, carefully, "Sometimes we don't let our-

selves believe things because we don't want to believe
them, you know. Perhaps your mother isn't trying to
fool you at all, Willet. Perhaps your father really is
dead, after all."

"He's not!" cried Willet. "I know he's not. Don't
you believe me? What I think we ought to do is go
and look for him. He's alive somewhere, I know he is,
and he must be lonesome. Listen, Hercules, the horse
never came back! Don't horses always come back, if
they've lost their riders? He didn't die and he isn't
down there in the tomb. We'll go down there and I'll
show you!" And he sprang to his feet.

Hercules leaped up in alarm. "We mustn't do that!
We can't do that! Look here—now, sit down and
listen." They both sat down again and Hercules took
Willet by the hand. "Give me some time to think
about it, Willet," he pleaded. "Perhaps I can find a
way—talk to people—there must have been someone
around at the time—someone who might know something that would help."

"Well, all right," said Willet, relaxing a little. "If
you want to. I guess we can't go looking for him if we
don't know where to start." He beamed at Hercules

happily. "Just think—the day before yesterday I was all alone except for Mama, with no one to talk to, and now you've come and you know everything and we're friends and as soon as we can we're going to go and find my father. Together." He settled himself against one leg of the iron stag and looked at Hercules with confident resignation. "All right. Let's get on with the lessons."

"Yes," said Hercules firmly. "Lessons. We'll begin with something really pleasant, like ornithology and botany. That's birds and flowers. A long walk in the woods would be just right for a day like today."

But Hercules Feltwright saw that nothing much was apt to come of lessons at Goody Hall. There was too much going on in the shadows. And in spite of Willet's certainty, he was himself not quite convinced. Was Midas Goody dead or wasn't he? For a moment the question seemed to settle heavily about his thin shoulders and he drooped under it. What kind of a thing was this, anyway, for a brand-new tutor to take on? And then suddenly he felt that it was an extremely important kind of thing. "If a man is going to be a good teacher," he said to himself, "he must learn to sit in strange classrooms." The thought made him feel shy and pleased and—determined. And all at once he knew what he was going to do. He was going to have a talk with the gardener, Alfresco Rom, and maybe even with Alfreida. "Alfresco's been down inside the tomb, or he couldn't have described it to Willet," he mused. "I'll just go round to his cottage tonight and explain the situation to him. Why, it must be a terrible thing to live all alone with doubts like Willet's, keeping them a secret and worrying about them all these years, even if he has had a beautiful house to do it in." He looked up at the house, and the house seemed to look back at him through all its polished windows. It looked back at him—somehow —smugly, as if it were saying, "None of that matters, anyway, you know. Not while they have me." And Hercules Feltwright felt for the first time, and felt foolish for feeling it, that the house was somehow to blame for all of Willet's troubles, but that the house was too proud—and too beautiful—to care.

CHAPTER 7

"Well, Dora, what's the news from Goody Hall?" asked the blacksmith as his sister came puffing into the shop with a market basket over her arm. "Did that strange-looking young man come by about the tutoring?"

Mrs. Tidings sank down on a nail keg and patted at her face with a small handkerchief. "Henry," she said solemnly, "Henry, I don't know where to begin, truly I don't!"

"Ah!" said the blacksmith with satisfaction. "I was right! I've been having this feeling that something was going to happen." He pulled up another nail keg and settled himself on it, leaning forward expectantly.

"Well!" said Mrs. Tidings. "First of all, that young man did come by. His name is Hercules Feltwright, of all outlandish things. And she hired him on the spot. On the *spot*, I tell you—with no questions asked. I didn't like the looks of him at first. Not that *she* noticed anything peculiar, of course. I unpacked his satchel for him and it was full of what looked like costumes. Play costumes. He wears them, too. You should have seen him at breakfast this morning."

"An actor, eh?" said the blacksmith, raising his eyebrows. "That's a new one. What does an actor know about tutoring?"

"I'm sure *I* don't know," said Mrs. Tidings. "He had a ratty old animal skin in his satchel, too. Most peculiar. So I said to her, I said, 'This person you've hired to be a tutor is a former actor.' And *she* said,

'How lovely! I always did like a play when I was a girl.' And then she packed up her bag and went off again up to the city without another word."

"Oho!" said the blacksmith. "Another trip to the city, eh?"

"Another trip," said Mrs. Tidings. She shook her head. "What *do* you suppose she does there? Twice a year, regular as clockwork, ever since Mr. Goody died."

The blacksmith stroked his beard and pondered. He and Mrs. Tidings had been over it all a hundred times, but they never tired of it.

"She comes back and she never has any packages with her," said Mrs. Tidings for the hundred-and-first time. "Not so much as a twist of brown paper in five years."

Again they pondered.

"It's very peculiar," said the blacksmith.

"It certainly is!" agreed his sister. And then she said importantly, "Last night this Feltwright had a visitor. A man all wrapped up in a cloak and scarf. I wouldn't let him in. I asked the young man about it this morning and he let slip that the fellow was probably after his money." She paused to let this announcement make its full impact and was pleased to see her brother's eyes widen. "It turns out, Henry, that the young man will be rich someday. He's got an aunt who's going to leave him everything. Now what do you think of that?"

The blacksmith sat back on his nail keg and whistled. "Well well! That explains a lot! He's one of these eccentric young lords, then, who go about the country to sow their oats before settling down to inherit their gold. I've heard of that kind of thing before. Well well!"

"Oh, he's a sly one, all right," said Mrs. Tidings. "Tried to put me off. But it's not that easy to fool Dora Tidings." She smirked a little and then added confidentially, "It occurs to me that he may be connected with the Goody family somehow. A cousin, perhaps. And that would explain why she hired him so quickly."

"Very likely, Dora," said the blacksmith with admiration. "Very likely." They nodded at each other happily.

"Well," said Mrs. Tidings, getting to her feet and

picking up the basket, "I'd better go on back to the Hall. I thought I'd fix something special for supper."

The blacksmith peered into her basket and sighed. "Beef and kidneys! And wine, too," he said longingly. "Nobody starves to death at Goody Hall." And then, just as his sister started out the door, he called her back. "Dora! Wait! I nearly forgot, with all the talk about young Feltwright's fortune. Did you say this visitor of his was all wrapped up in a cloak and scarf?"

"Yes, I did," said Mrs. Tidings. "And he had a hat on, too."

"Then I've seen the fellow!" the blacksmith announced, proud to have news of his own to report. "I've seen him. I was closing up the shop last evening when he went by across the street. I said to myself at the time that it was a funny way to dress on a warm night. A red scarf?"

"That's it," said Mrs. Tidings. "Young Feltwright told me his name was . . . now, let me see . . . Stave? Shave? No—Snave. That's what it was. Mott Snave. But he told me this morning that he'd never met him. Mott Snave. I haven't heard the name before. And you say you saw him here in the village?"

"Last night," said the blacksmith. "He must have been on his way to the Hall at the time."

"So he must," said Mrs. Tidings. "How very peculiar! A red scarf and a long black cloak?"

"The very man himself," said the blacksmith. "I'll keep a weather eye out for him, shall I?"

"Yes indeed," said Mrs. Tidings. "By all means. Well! It looks to be an interesting summer!"

"That's the truth," said the blacksmith contentedly. "That's the truth."

And Mrs. Tidings hummed a little tune all the way back to Goody Hall.

CHAPTER 8

At dusk it began to rain. Not one of your misty spring rains that whisper for a few minutes and then move off, but a hard, determined downpour, a real gully-washer that hung over the twilit countryside like smoke. Hercules Feltwright was not to be put off from his plans by a little weather, however. He fetched a wide-brimmed hat from his room and, enriched by beef and kidneys and heartened by wine, he stood before Mrs. Tidings and announced his intentions. "Willet is in bed," he said firmly, "and I'm going out. I have some business in the village."

Mrs. Tidings nodded sweetly. "Very well, Mr. Feltwright," she said. "Going in to meet that fellow Snave, I suppose?"

Hercules frowned. "No," he said. "Not at all."

"No? Then—going to post a letter to your aunt, perhaps."

"No letters," said Hercules.

"Oh," said Mrs. Tidings. "Well, then . . ."

"Never mind," said Hercules. "It's business. Nothing interesting."

Mrs. Tidings gave up. "Very well," she said, a little reproachfully. "You'll need an umbrella." And she brought him one, a large black one with a curved horn handle. "Try to stay dry," she advised. "It's a bad night." And then she added hopefully, "Shall I wait up for you?"

"Certainly not," he said hastily, trying hard not to sound rude. And he hurried out the door.

The rain made waterfalls all around him as he went down the dim path and through the gate, and pounded on the black bowl of the umbrella as if it wanted to come in out of itself. But Hercules Feltwright didn't mind. In fact, he enjoyed it. A big umbrella was the coziest thing in the world—he had always thought so—and the harder it rained, the cozier it was. He grasped the horn handle firmly and turned down the road toward the village. His feet in their aging socks and loose, buttoned shoes were wet almost at once, but he didn't mind that, either. He sloshed along quite happily in the streaming dark, thinking of what he was going to say to Alfresco Rom, and listening to the splash and rattle of the rain in the trees along the road.

After a while he began to talk out loud to himself. "I'll say, 'See here, Rom, you've got to help me.' No, that won't do. I'd better say, 'Mr. Rom, I need your assistance.' And then I'll say, 'Willet Goody believes his father is still alive. Willet is very unhappy. In my capacity as his tutor, it is my responsibility to look after his mental well-being.' No—that sounds pompous. Better put it simply. 'It's bad for the boy to go on worrying about his father in this fashion and

we've got to help him. You must know something.' "
Here his thoughts began to wander a little. "The
horse never came back . . . clank . . . nobody in
the coffin at all . . . and she was never even sad
. . . Midas Goody has a big nose . . . clank . . .
why did it go *clank?* . . . oof!" He tripped over a
tree root in the dark and barely saved himself from
falling by flipping the umbrella over and catching
himself with it as if it were a cane. Of course, he was
soaked from head to foot at once, as the rain seized
him at last; but he stood unheeding for a moment,
leaning on the umbrella and thinking about Goody
Hall while water filled his hat brim and began to form
a little pool in the inverted umbrella. Then he swept
it up over his head again, paying no attention as the
pool spilled down the back of his neck. "I've got to
find out," he said to himself. "I've got to be absolutely
sure about Midas Goody. And then I'll know how to
help Willet, one way or the other." And he splashed
off, stern and determined.

The cottage of Alfresco Rom and his daughter Alfreida stood at the very edge of the village in a lit-

tle grove of dripping birches. Hercules might have missed it altogether if it hadn't been for a small white sign tacked to a post at the roadside. "*Séances!*" the sign announced with enthusiasm. "*Inquire Within.*" Hercules turned off the road and waded through an enormous puddle up to a small porch, where he furled the umbrella and rapped on the cottage door. Alfreida opened it almost at once and peered out. "Why, hello there, dearie," she said. "Come on in out of the rain."

Hercules stepped inside and found himself standing in a small room brightly lit with candles and crowded with odds and ends of elderly furniture. Everything was draped and dramatized in bright colors—beaded cushions were tossed here and there, and large wild scarves were spread across the backs of chairs and over the tops of tables. There was a tall pot of dried flowers standing inside the fireplace, and another on the floor beside a sagging sofa upholstered in worn but by no means discouraged red plush.

Alfreida didn't seem at all surprised to see him. She made a cordial gesture toward the sofa and said, "Sit down, dearie. I'll make a pot of tea."

"I'm wet," said Hercules unnecessarily. Water was

running from him everywhere, and a puddle began to form around his feet.

Alfreida looked at him and shook her head. "Imagine that!" she said. "Never mind. Nobody's going to bother over a little rain water here. This is home, you know, not Goody Hall."

Hercules looked around at the odd but friendly room and nodded in a pleased kind of way. "That's true!" he said, and sat down. The sofa groaned under him and he stood up again hastily. "You see," he explained, "I came to see your father. Do you think he'd be willing to talk to me?"

"I don't know, dearie," said Alfreida. "I'll ask him." And she opened a door at the back of the room and disappeared through it.

Hercules sat down again on the sofa, carefully, and waited, wriggling his feet. His socks had drooped into the tops of his shoes and were forming soggy lumps under his toes, but he wasn't thinking about his socks. He was thinking about Willet. After a few minutes, during which, all unaware, he had set up a rhythmic *squish-squish* by rocking his feet inside the wet shoes, he heard a grumbling voice and Alfresco Rom stumped into the room. The old man wore a very alarming scowl and the first thing he said was, "What's that squishing noise?"

Hercules, feeling suddenly timid and foolish, traced the trouble at once to his own feet and stilled them. He cleared his throat and stood up. "Mr. Rom," he began, "I need your assistance."

Alfresco's scowl deepened. "Well?" he rasped. "What is it?"

Hercules cleared his throat again. "Well, you see, sir," he said haltingly, "it's about Willet Goody. Willet thinks . . . that is, Willet has been telling me . . ." And then, all in a rush, with his eyes shut and wondering whether Alfresco would strike him down with the poker: "Willet claims his father isn't dead at all—that there's nobody in the tomb—and he worries about it all the time—and that isn't good for him—and I just thought maybe you could tell me something that would . . . help." It was out, and after a moment he opened his eyes to see whether Alfresco had picked up the poker yet.

But Alfresco was only standing there scowling at

him out of narrowed black eyes. "Why does the boy think his father isn't dead?" he growled.

"Well—because—it sounds a little silly, maybe, but it *isn't* silly, Mr. Rom, when a child has worries like this—he thinks so because Mrs. Goody was never even sad, and the horse didn't come back, and most of all, the coffin went clank."

"The coffin did what?" said Alfresco, scowling more than ever.

"It went . . . clank," said Hercules, and somebody giggled nervously. It took him a moment to realize that he had done the giggling himself. He blushed and cleared his throat for a third time. "Look here, Mr. Rom, I only thought if you were there when it happened, you might be able to tell me something that would help."

"I was there," said Alfresco. The scowl remained about his mouth but his black eyes were suddenly bleak, remembering. "It was a bad business. I carried the coffin down into the tomb myself, me and a couple of fellows who were passing by on the road. Wasn't anybody else there except for the women. And the old parson. He's gone now." The bleakness left his eyes and he scowled so deeply that his moustache quivered. "I'd just as soon help that boy, but there's nothing I can do. You'd better go."

At that moment Alfreida came back into the room carrying a tray with a teapot and three cups. "Don't go yet, dearie," she said to Hercules. "The tea's just ready. Sit down, Father, and have a cup of tea."

Alfresco stood there staring at Hercules. The bleak look had come into his eyes again, and he rubbed the back of his neck with one worn old hand. "There's nothing I can do," he repeated, a little uncertainly. And then he closed his eyes. "I'm tired. I'm going to bed." And he turned and stumped out of the room, closing the door behind him.

"I heard it all," said Alfreida comfortably. "Sit down, dearie. I heard it all while I was making the tea. My father doesn't like to talk about Midas Goody. He'd have left that work out there long ago if it weren't for the fact that it's really his garden. He made it all. Wasn't a thing there but a field before the Goodys built that silly house, and my father did all the clearing and planting. He loves that garden. Here's your tea." She sat back and stirred her own cup. "He won't tell you anything," she said. "But remember what I said to you yesterday—if you want to know something about somebody who's dead, you ought to ask *me*."

"You?" said Hercules.

"That's right, dearie. If you want to know how Midas Goody died, I'll call him back for you and you can ask him yourself."

Hercules Feltwright took a sip of tea. "Here I am," he thought, "sitting here calmly drinking tea with a round little woman in the middle of a rainstorm and in a minute we're going to talk to the dead." The notion made his stomach feel hollow. "Well!" he said out loud with false heartiness. "There's an idea!"

Alfreida put down her cup, stood up, and began walking around the room blowing out candles. Hercules took a large swallow of tea and nearly choked. "What are you doing that for?" he quavered.

"Can't have a séance in broad daylight," said Alfreida cheerfully. She left two candles burning on a small table which she placed in front of him, but the rest of the room was lost in shadows. "Sit there and enjoy your tea," she said, "while I get ready. I'll only be a minute." And she left the room.

Hercules sat there on the sofa in the dimness and listened to the rain drumming on the roof. He was very conscious now of his wet socks. He rocked his feet. *Squish-squish*. "Good grief!" he said to himself miserably.

Then Alfreida was back, and he felt a wild desire to giggle again. She was wrapped in a long dark robe of some sort that made her look rounder than ever, and on her head she wore a turban in violent shades of green and orange, with trembling yellow fringe. But her face was composed and confident. She pulled up a chair opposite him and from under the robe produced a small crystal ball on a wooden base, which she set on the table between them. "You'll have to be very quiet, dearie," she warned. "I can't go into a trance if there's noise." She placed her stubby fingers around the ball and closed her eyes.

There was a long, long minute of silence. The

rain continued, harder than ever, and the candles flickered. Hercules folded his hands to keep them from shaking and watched the shadowy face before him. Suddenly, so suddenly that he jumped, her hands fell away from the crystal ball and lay loose and relaxed on the tabletop. She drooped a little in the chair and then her eyes opened and looked directly at him, but he knew at once that she wasn't seeing him at all. Her mouth opened slightly and she made a strange sort of noise, somewhere between a laugh and a moan. Hercules felt the short hairs on the back of his neck begin to prickle and his throat went tight and dry.

When Alfreida spoke, it wasn't with her normal voice at all. She looked right at him with empty black eyes and she said gruffly, "Well, what do you want?"

Hercules tried to answer, swallowed, tried again, and managed to squeak out: "I want to speak to Midas Goody!"

"Somebody here wants to speak to *you* first," said the gruff voice coming out of Alfreida's mouth. There was a brief silence and then a new, higher voice spoke.

"If you're going to go around quoting me, for pity's sake do it properly!" said the new voice waspishly. "If there's anything I can't abide, it's to be misquoted."

Hercules Feltwright's mouth dropped open. "What?" he goggled. "Who's that?"

The voice ignored his question. "You actors are all alike," it complained. "Always trying to improve on the play. 'Where the sea bucks,' indeed! 'Where the *bee sucks*,' you ninny!"

"I—I'm sorry," said Hercules. He simply could not believe what he was hearing, and yet—there it was. He was certainly hearing it.

"Where the *bee sucks*," said the voice from farther away, and then there was another, longer silence. Hercules sat red-eared, badly shaken by this last voice, and watched Alfreida's face nervously. At last, just as he was deciding with relief that there wouldn't be any more, the gruff voice suddenly returned. "Midas Goody?"

"Yes," said Hercules, forgetting the other voice. He thought of Willet and began to hope.

"When did he cross over?" the gruff voice inquired.

"Cross over? Oh! *Er*—five years ago. He fell off his horse," said Hercules, feeling eager and helpful.

Again there was a long silence. Hercules rocked his feet. *Squish-squish*. Then the gruff voice was back again. "No," it said firmly.

"No?" said Hercules.

"No," said the voice. "Nobody here by that name from that time in that manner. Nobody."

Hercules sat forward. "But if he isn't there, then he isn't . . ."

"He hasn't crossed over yet," said the voice. "If he had, he'd be here. He isn't here. So he didn't cross over." The voice began to fade. "He didn't cross over," it repeated faintly, and then it sighed and faded away altogether. Silence again. At last Alfreida's hands, lying on the table, began to twitch. Her eyes closed. A deep shudder shook her and then suddenly she was herself again. The séance was over.

Alfreida sat up briskly and took off the turban. "Whee-ooo!" she said. "Well! How did it go, dearie? Did you talk to Midas Goody?"

Hercules stood up slowly and started for the door. "No, I didn't," he said. "He wasn't there." He picked up the umbrella.

"Well now!" said Alfreida, standing up. "What do you know about that?"

Hercules peered at her. Her black eyes mocked him and the gold tooth winked. He stepped out onto the little porch and opened the umbrella. The pouring rain roared in his ears. "Thank you," he said vaguely. And then he looked at her again, possessed by sudden doubt.

Alfreida came to the door. She raised her eyebrows. "What's the matter, dearie?" she said with false concern. "Don't you believe what you heard?" And then she gave him a taunting laugh and shut the door firmly between them.

Hercules stood alone on the little porch and listened to the rain. "I wonder," he said to himself. "I wonder if I do believe it."

CHAPTER 9

There's something about spring—or, at least, spring in the morning after a good night's rain —that makes a problem seem less troublesome. Hercules Feltwright stuck his head out of his bedroom window and sniffed. The morning sky was washed clean of clouds and the lilac bush looked especially vigorous. An early-rising bee circled briskly among the blossoms. In the yard below, the iron stag was

studded with shining drops of rain water where the
sun had not yet touched it. "This is the kind of day,"
said Hercules to himself, "to get things done in. If I
knew what to do, that is." He pulled in his head and
began to dress himself. One thing was clear—he
knew what *not* to do. He would not tell Willet about
the séance. Not yet, at least. He wanted to think about
it first. After all—a séance! That voice, complaining
about actors. What kind of a thing was that, anyway?
He wasn't at all sure he believed in it, with the morning sun streaming in through the window.

After breakfast—and a neat turning aside of
several questions from Mrs. Tidings—it was time
again for lessons. "The thing is," said Hercules to
Willet, "I don't know how much you've learned already. And I have to find that out before I know what
to teach you." Willet looked at him expectantly.
"So," said Hercules, "we'll start with spelling. I want
you to go all through the house and write down a
list of the things you see. You know, like chair, table,
window. And then I'll check it over and see if you've
spelled them all correctly."

"All right," said Willet. "Where shall I begin?"

"Well," said Hercules, "why don't you begin up-stairs? That's as good a place as any."

Willet went off happily and Hercules sat down in the parlor to think about the séance. But somehow, concentration seemed difficult. He turned his head uneasily, wondering why, and found himself looking into the world-weary eyes of a small marble statue that stood on a delicate little table at his elbow. The statue was of a superior-looking gentleman in a toga who lounged on a sort of stool—or perhaps it was a tree stump—looking bored and graceful. Hercules caught himself trying, involuntarily, to ar-range his legs in their baggy trousers to match the position of the statue, and stopped at once in annoy-ance. "If this house had its way," he thought, "it would make me over into a regular dandy." He turned the statue around so it couldn't watch him any more, and settled down again to think. But the room in which he sat was very elegant. It pressed on him. It insisted. And before he knew it, his thoughts had drifted into another fantasy like the one at the gate on the very first day. The room filled with shadowy ladies of fashion in bobbing headdresses and he himself, in immaculate evening clothes, stood carelessly among them, smoking a large cigar. "Yes, yes," he heard himself say, "it's a great burden to be so wealthy, but what can one do?" And the ladies of fashion all murmured sympathetically.

"Did you say something?" asked a voice. The scene vanished with the silent pop of a soap bubble and he found that Mrs. Tidings was standing in the doorway looking at him curiously.

"No, no," he answered hastily, collecting himself. "I was just . . . thinking."

Mrs. Tidings came into the parlor and began whisking at the tops of things with an enormous feather duster. "This is a fine room," she said companionably. "But then, I suppose you're accustomed to fine rooms."

"Oh no, not at all," he said, thinking guiltily of his penny-saving aunt. Very deliberately, he reached inside his shirt and scratched loosely at his stomach. It was the un-finest gesture he could think of at the moment.

Mrs. Tidings ignored it. She picked up the statue

of the superior-looking gentleman and dusted it carefully. "That's Mr. Goody's chair you're sitting in," she observed. "He was sitting in it the day before he died." She sighed and replaced the statue so that it gazed again in Hercules' direction. "Poor Mr. Goody! And him so young and all! He wasn't more than thirty-five or -six when the accident happened, you know."

It occurred to Hercules that there were probably a great many things Mrs. Tidings could tell him that he really needed to know. He said, trying to sound casual, "Were you here at the time?"

"Oh yes," said Mrs. Tidings, gazing upward in a pious manner. "Indeed I was! They carried him in from up the road where the horse threw him. Late one night, it was. Some people going by on their way to the city—they found him and brought him here. I couldn't bear to look at him, poor man."

"How did they know where to bring him?" asked Hercules curiously.

"Why, it seems to me they said there was someone else who came along who knew where he belonged—I really don't remember." She pressed a hand to her heart. "I ran into the kitchen and hid my face, you know, when they carried him in. But *she*—I mean, Mrs. Goody—she was as calm as you please about it after the first shock. And in two days he was in his tomb. Sad. Very sad." She sat down on a little gilded chair across from Hercules and looked at him approvingly, and then she gazed at the ceiling again. "It was a blessing in a way," she said. "One of the people who found him turned out to be a doctor. He signed the death certificate and sent off the notices to the registrar and everything."

"Was there a large funeral?" asked Hercules.

"Dear me, no. They hadn't any friends at all, you see," said Mrs. Tidings. "Always kept to themselves. No, just a few words at the tomb. The old parson read the service. He's gone now. And that's all there was to it. Boom bang—it was over. Here one day and gone the next." She plucked at the feather duster, looking solemn.

"But then, I suppose," said Hercules carefully, "Mrs. Goody mourned for a long time."

Mrs. Tidings closed her eyes. "Well!" she said. "It's not my place to make observations about my employer. But since you ask, it didn't seem to me she was a bit sorry. Not a bit!" She opened her eyes again and looked at him severely.

"Still," said Hercules, "he *was* dead, wasn't he, just the same."

"Oh, indeed he was," said Mrs. Tidings. "And *is*, poor man."

Just at that moment Willet called from the hall upstairs. "Hercules! Hercules, come up! I . . . I need you."

Hercules left Mrs. Tidings with a sigh of relief and hurried up the stairs. "What is it?" he asked. "Did you find something you don't know how to spell?"

But it wasn't that at all. Willet stood waiting for him in a doorway at the end of the hall and his face was pink with excitement. "Come here!" he whispered. "I just found something!"

The doorway where Willet was waiting opened into an elaborate bedroom full of carved, curly furniture upholstered in satin and velvet and smothered with embroidered cushions. The carpet was a garden of rich, woven flowers and birds, and the mantelpiece was crowded with china figurines.

"This is my mother's bedroom," said Willet in a low voice.

"Dear me!" said Hercules. "We shouldn't be in here!"

"Sh-h-h!" whispered Willet. "I don't want Mrs. Tidings to know what we're doing. I'm not allowed to come in here, but I thought it wouldn't matter for just a few minutes. There are a lot of good things in here to spell. So I came in and I went and sat down on that footstool over there—"

"That's a hassock," said Hercules.

"—on that hassock over there, and I guess I sat too close to the edge because it turned over and I ended up on the floor, and when I went to set it up again I noticed something funny—well, come and see for yourself!"

The hassock lay upside down on the carpet and there was a hole in its wooden bottom, a hole fitted with a little hinged door which now stood open. Hercules peered into the hole. Something winked up

at him. He reached inside, fished around, and came
up with a dazzling handful of loose jewels. Diamonds,
a few emeralds, rubies, and sapphires, and several
other stones he didn't recognize. Some were cut and
polished and others were still rough. "What in the
world is this?" he gasped, staring at the gleaming
little mound in his hand.

"Why, it's jewels, Hercules!" whispered Willet.
"Lots and lots of jewels! Aren't they beautiful?
Where do you suppose she got them?"

"Well, your father was a very rich man, you
know," said Hercules in an awed voice. "They're
beautiful, all right. Why, there's enough here to . . .
to choke a horse."

"I wonder why she keeps them in this old footstool," whispered Willet.

"Hassock," said Hercules, "and we'd better put
them back before someone finds us here." He dumped
the shining pile back into the hole, closed the little
door, and turned the hassock upright again. And he
was just in time—someone was clumping up the
stairs. They hurried to the door, but it was too late
to escape. Alfreida was coming down the hall with an

armload of folded bedsheets, and she saw them at once.

"Well, well!" she said. "All dried out this morning, Mr. Feltwright? What are you doing in there?"

"We're playing a spelling game," said Hercules heartily. "Curtain, Willet. C-U-R-T-A-I-N."

"I'm glad to see you're paying some attention to your tutoring," said Alfreida, "but you're not supposed to tute in Mrs. Goody's bedroom. No one's allowed in Mrs. Goody's bedroom except to change the sheets. So you'd better go and tute somewhere else."

"Bugfat," said Willet. "This is my house and I guess I can go where I want to in it."

"It isn't your house," said Alfreida calmly. "It's your mother's house. And your mother says no one's allowed in her bedroom except to change the sheets."

"Never mind," said Hercules. "We were just going out anyway. Come along, Willet—we'll try some spelling words outside. Lilac, for instance— L-I-L-A-C."

Alfreida put down her load of sheets on a table in

the hall. "If you want a really hard word, dearie," she grinned, "how about séance? S-E-A-N-C-E."

Hercules hurried Willet down the stairs without replying, but they could hear Alfreida chuckling as she went about her work.

The sun had dried the iron stag's smooth hide by now and the grass around its hooves smelled rich and fragrant. Hercules and Willet went there to sit side by side in what had become their own special spot. Hercules glanced at Willet and then rubbed his forehead ruefully. "Webs within webs!" he said. "Now it's jewels hidden in a hassock! And yet," he added, "I suppose it isn't really so strange after all. She wouldn't just leave them lying about, a fortune like that. They're probably old family jewels, you know. Handed down from father to son. It's odd they've never been set into bracelets or something, though, isn't it?" Willet said nothing, so he went on chattily. "It's very possible your mother has been selling them off—to keep going, you know. I wouldn't be at all surprised if that's what she does when she goes to the city. Although I can't see why she'd want to keep it a

secret from *you*. They'll all be yours someday, anyway, if there are any left by that time." Still Willet
said nothing. "Of course, they'd last a whole lot
longer," Hercules observed, "if there wasn't such a
big house to keep up and Mrs. Tidings to pay and all,
but I suppose if one is used to living grandly, it would
be hard to change. Well, it's a good thing Mott Snave
isn't really anywhere about! He'd love to sneak off
with a treasure like that."

And still Willet was silent, pulling at the grass
between his knees.

"All right," said Hercules, "I know what you're
thinking, but it isn't like that at all."

Willet looked at him reproachfully. "You went to
see Alfreida last night, didn't you? And you didn't
tell me."

Hercules sighed. "I didn't want to say anything
about it yet. I don't know quite what to make of it
all."

"Did you ask her if she knew anything about my
father?" Willet demanded.

"Well, you see, I went to see Alfresco, really, but

he acted a little queer. He didn't seem to want to talk. And then Alfreida—Alfreida suggested a séance."

"A séance? Why?"

"That's the part I didn't want to tell you about until I'd had time to think it over," said Hercules. "I would have told you sooner or later—it's just that at the moment I'm not sure what there is to tell."

Willet looked accusing. "It's *my* father after all, Hercules. Tell me what happened."

"Well, all right. But it won't be much help. You see, Alfreida thought that she could call your father back and I could talk to him." Willet frowned, but sat silent. "There was a voice," Hercules continued. "I don't know whether it was real or not. It said that your father hadn't—that is, that he isn't dead."

Color rushed into Willet's cheeks. "But that's what I've been saying all along!" he cried. "I *told* you, Hercules!"

"I know, Willet. But a séance—it doesn't prove anything, really."

"What you mean is, you didn't believe the voice."

"Well—I did for a while, but now I'm not so sure. Alfreida may have made the whole thing up, just to fool me."

"But why would she want to do that?"

Hercules frowned. "I don't know. I can't think why. The thing is, Willet, I have to be sure. I hope you're right about your father. I *want* you to be right. But the clank in the coffin and all, and the séance—that's just not enough to send you and me wandering off in all directions looking for a man who may not want to be found, even if he *is* alive."

"Well then," said Willet helplessly, "what are you going to *do?*"

"I don't know yet," said Hercules.

But he did. Without ever being conscious of it, he had in fact made up his mind. He looked across the lawn at the hedge behind the garden. He couldn't see the tomb through the thick leaves, but the slender upper branches of the poplars that surrounded it beckoned to him over the top of the hedge, and he knew what he had to do.

CHAPTER 10

Hercules Feltwright took out his nose putty and squeezed it. Outside, the moon blinked through drifting shreds of cloud, and the lilac bush scratched against his window as a stiff night breeze circled the beautiful house. Hercules pressed the putty over his nose and was annoyed to see that his hands were shaking a little. "After all, though," he thought defensively, "it isn't exactly what I expected in the line of tutoring duty." The nose was in place at last, as much like the first one as he could manage, and he went to the wardrobe and swung open its double doors. "Acting was simpler," he observed to himself as he took out the vest and cloak and put them on. "It's much easier to talk about doing things than it is to really do them. Why, I've been through all kinds of horrors on stage, without a quiver. For instance, that terrible murder, all pretend, of course, and then I come out and I say:

"*Friends, Romans, countrymen, send me your fears.*
I come to harry Caesar, not to raise him.
The evils that ensue . . ."

He stopped suddenly, remembering the voice in Alfreida's parlor. "Or *something* like that," he ended lamely, listening over his shoulder as if he half expected the waspish voice to come out of nowhere and correct him again. But nothing happened. Reassured, he wrapped the long red scarf around his neck and chin, and put on the flat black hat. "There!" he said to his muffled reflection in the mirror. "If someone catches you at this dreadful business, they won't know it's you. I hope."

And still he lingered at the mirror, adjusting and readjusting the scarf, and patting at the putty nose until at last, from the next room, he heard Willet turn over and sigh in his sleep. "Willet!" he thought. "I'm doing it for Willet. To settle this question once and for all." And so he straightened his shoulders, picked up matches and a candle, and in the soundless, prowling step he imagined for the thief Mott Snave, he glided out of the room and down the stairs.

Outside, on the dim and shadowy lawn, the breeze wrapped the cloak tight around his knees and then flung it out behind him, and the ends of the scarf danced. He stood there, his knees glued with reluctance, and then an idea occurred to him. "Perhaps the entrance will be sealed shut. Yes, of course it will be. Why didn't I think of that long ago? Well, I guess there's really no point in . . ." But just as he was about to turn back to the house, he thought again of Willet and was ashamed of himself. "Forward!" he commanded desperately, and marched himself across the grass toward the hedge.

In the garden, the tulips nodded stiffly. They looked gray and black and rather dead in the gloom. Hercules stepped around them with care and confronted the hedge. Now, where was that spot where you could squeeze through without scratching yourself to bits? Oh yes, here it was, over here. And he forced his way through the probing branches and stood at last, cloak and scarf and tip of nose askew, on the other side.

The poplars which had beckoned to him earlier whispered now—*ahh-h-h!*—and bowed their heads, and the moon chose that moment to slip free of a claw of clouds. In the sudden glow, the small square building, the tomb of Midas Goody, loomed before him and it was like the last grim stepping-stone of life.

Everything that had ever happened to Hercules Feltwright before this instant receded from his memory as he stood there looking at the tomb. Every love, every joy, and every happy purpose drained away. He felt weightless and brittle, like the paper shell of some long-dead insect, and the hand that reached out to the door seemed to belong to somebody else. But the wood pressing back at his fingers was real enough. It was cool and rough to the touch, and when he pushed against it, it moved with alarming ease, swung inward, and hung open over what appeared to be a chasm of darkness. Then in the moonlight he was able to make out the beginning of a flight of stone steps. "This is it," he croaked to himself. "Here it is, the descent into Hell, and I'm going down. I, Hercules Feltwright, am going down."

Inside, on the top step out of the wind, he paused and with trembling fingers lit the candle he had brought along. The sudden light was blinding at first. He held it up and stood under it, sheltered from the dark as, the night before, he had stood under the umbrella. Then he realized that he was moving forward. "I really *am* going down!" he said in horrified surprise.

Afterward he realized that there were only a few steps, six or seven, but now it seemed as if the tomb were bottomless, as if he were going deeper and deeper into the very center of the earth, ten feet, ten miles deep with every step. The light of the candle, which had been so brilliant at the top, now seemed to

shrink pitifully to no more than a glow he could hold
in one hand, the feeble pinpoint of a lightning bug.
And then, after an hour, after a year, he was at the
bottom of the steps, and before him, on a slab of
stone, lay the coffin of Midas Goody.

Hercules Feltwright stood absolutely still, gazing
at the coffin, aware by degrees of the coldness of the
air, the flat, clammy coldness that had been five years
hanging there without a breath to stir it. The candle
flickered and he realized that he was staring so hugely
that his lids ached. He wondered then if his eyes
might not fall out, and shut them hastily. When he
opened them again, the coffin was still there. "It's
waiting," he told himself, "waiting for *me*."

From somewhere deep in his horrified brain a
reasonable question formed: "Why you? It's nothing
to do with you, not really. Take off that silly nose and
run. Run!" But he didn't run. Instead, he summoned
every ounce of courage from every corner of himself
—from his knees, his thumbs, the soles of his feet—
and he said aloud, "Bugfat!" It seemed to help. Moving stiffly, he bent over and stood the candle against
the moist stones of the wall, where it hissed a little,

sending black streaks of soot up the wall like ink spilled upside down; and after observing this interesting phenomenon for a moment, he straightened and looked again at the coffin. With the candle on the floor now, the shadows had shifted. His own hung swollen down the far wall of the little room, and the coffin, lit from below, seemed twice as large. He walked slowly up to it, as you walk toward the edge of a cliff, and laid his hands on the lid. "Now!" he said to himself. But his muscles paid no attention. "Now!" he said again, more firmly. "I'm standing at the very Gates of Hell—and I'm going to *open*—NOW!"

With a great wrench, and a cracking of the old wax seals, he heaved, and the lid of the coffin flew open. And Hercules Feltwright stood staring, not at the rotted wrappings and indignant bones of Midas Goody, but at the stiff silver grins of three dogs' heads, the three-headed, tarnished gleam of the silver statue of Cerberus.

If you cracked open your morning egg and found a book of poetry inside, if you lifted the top from a candy box and found instead of candy a bowl of water complete with goldfish, you would know, somewhat, how Hercules Feltwright felt in the tomb of Midas Goody. The first crazy thought that came into his head was that his mother had been there before him and had hidden the Cerberus statue, knowing he would come down and find it. He looked around the gloomy cubicle angrily, fully expecting her to step out of a corner and congratulate him. But no one was there. And then he thought, "It's impossible. I'm dreaming the whole thing." But the statue was real. And unless there were somehow two of them, which seemed very unlikely, it was Mott Snave's Cerberus, the bishop's Cerberus, exactly as it had always been described to him. He leaned heavily against the coffin, rubbing his eyes, and as he leaned, the coffin moved sidewise slightly and the statue, which stood a little unsteadily on its four silver legs, went *clank*.

Clank. "It went clank!" cried Hercules. "It did! It did!" And all at once, in a great rush, his blood seemed to leap again in his veins. His hands, so cold before, went hot, and his toes tingled. He seized the candle joyfully and, without bothering to replace the lid of the coffin, ran up the stone steps and out into the fresh dark night. The breeze snatched at him and the candle was puffed out, but Hercules Feltwright didn't care. He was full of a wild exultation. "I'll wake up Willet right away," he promised himself breathlessly. "I'll wake him and tell him he was right. Oops, the door—I almost forgot the door!" He hurried back and pulled it shut, found that he had shut it on the end of his scarf, opened it again, freed the scarf, and then again he shut it. He was through the hedge in a burst and standing on the lawn of the beautiful house, pausing to catch his breath, before it struck him: "But—good grief! That really *was* Mott Snave's statue of Cerberus in Midas Goody's coffin! How in the name of heaven did it get there?" And then, as if a switch had been thrown, his blood froze again on the instant. For there, not three yards away from him, and staring out at him from under the brim of another flat black hat, stood another shadowy figure wrapped in cloak and obscuring scarf, another figure so exactly like his own that for a moment he thought he was staring into a mirror. The other figure paused for an instant, and he thought he heard it whisper, "Ye gods!" And then, in a swirl of wind-tossed cloak, it turned and melted away into the darkness.

CHAPTER 11

If sleep were a willing guest you could invite as if
to a party, how easy nights like that one would
be. "Look here now," said Hercules Feltwright to his
spinning brain, "the thing to do is quiet down and
get some rest." But he might as well have ordered
a mosquito to stop humming. And anyway, he didn't
really want to sleep. He wanted to rush into Willet's
room and wake him up and tell him everything. But

how could he tell about having seen another Mott Snave in the dark? How could he possibly explain that? How could he explain how he had stood stunned on the lawn instead of rushing after the fellow, seizing him, forcing him to give himself up? There was a connection, of course, between the Cerberus in the coffin and Mott Snave on the lawn. There had to be. But how? He couldn't puzzle it out—he was too dumfounded—and so he had crept up to his room, put away the nose and the costume, and fumbled his way into nightshirt and bed without troubling even to light a candle. And now he lay there with his eyes shut, in one of his most dependable sleeping positions, and tried to pretend that he was drowsy.

But the moment he relaxed his grip on his thoughts, off they swooped again. Over and over he traced his own steps down into the tomb, over and over he opened the coffin and discovered the grinning heads of Cerberus, and over and over he saw before him on the shadowed lawn his twin in cape and scarf. Every swoop was a question, and every question a tangle without beginning or end. He could not even begin to guess how the statue came to be in the coffin, or how Mott Snave, if it was the real Mott Snave, came to be at Goody Hall.

Hercules Feltwright tried to force the turmoil out of his head. He lay there and imagined that his brain was a tiny room presided over by a little man with a broom. The tiny room was cluttered with thoughts which lay about on the floor, heaving like snakes. The little man opened a door, swept the thoughts out, and slammed the door on them, leaning against it, while the thoughts, gibbering and protesting, pushed hard from the other side. But the little man was too strong for them—they couldn't get back in. Hercules sighed with relief. This was a favorite system of his. It always worked. Then, as he lay there, he remembered Alfreida and her séance. And thinking about Alfreida, he remembered Alfresco. He sat bolt upright in bed. "Alfresco *does* know what happened!" he said, with sudden certainty. "I'll ask him in the morning." The certainty was like the blowing out of a candle. His mind emptied, his knees loosened. He fell back on the pillow and went instantly to sleep.

To be sure, he dreamed. And in his dreams Mott Snave and Alfreida and Willet and Mrs. Tidings were all dancing a fandango, the three heads of Cerberus sang a charming trio, and he himself, draped in a lion's skin, was cavorting with the superior-looking gentleman from the parlor table, who, though much enlarged and certainly a marble statue in a toga, was surprisingly graceful and lithe. From the sidelines his mother beamed fondly and kept saying, "Hero! Hero!" The result of all this was that he woke up in the morning very tired indeed but somehow extremely pleased with himself.

Breakfast seemed to take forever, but when at last it was over, Hercules Feltwright seized Willet by the hand, pulled him out of the house and over to the iron stag, and sat him down in the dewy grass in such a hurry that Willet, who was still chewing on a final muffin, nearly choked with surprise.

"What's the matter, Hercules?" he managed through a mouthful. "What's happened?"

And Hercules, plumping down beside him, told him at last everything that had happened the night before. "So you see, Willet," he said when the tale was done, "that's the final proof. Your father is definitely not in the coffin, and instead of that solving the puzzle, or untangling any webs, it all looks more tangled than ever. *But*—Alfresco knows the answers. I'm sure of it. And the very next thing to do is to find him and make him tell us."

Willet sat breathless on the grass, his eyes wide and shining, torn between joy and confusion. "A silver statue in the coffin!" he said. "That explains the clanking noise."

"It clanked last night!" Hercules put in. "I leaned against the coffin and it clanked."

"Well, it looks as if the Mott Snave stories are true after all," said Willet grudgingly. "You were right, Hercules. But what was he doing here? Maybe he put the statue in the coffin himself. Do you suppose that's it?"

"I haven't the least idea," said Hercules. "It's a real poser. And . . . there's another thing. Mrs. Tidings told me yesterday that the night your father was killed, *supposedly* killed, some people brought the body back here to Goody Hall. She saw it. She didn't look closely at it, but she saw it. *Somebody* died that night, Willet, and the question is—who?" They stared at each other and then Hercules said, "Well, we're going to find out, that's what we're going to do. And we're going to find out now. Come on. We'll look for Alfresco. He must be somewhere about."

Behind the beautiful house, and masked somewhat by a thick curtain of wisteria, stood a small shed, and inside the shed, laying out his tools for the day from the rakes and clippers and other implements that lined its walls, they did indeed find Alfresco Rom. "Well?" he barked when he saw them. "What do you want?" His wrinkled brown face scowled and he turned an angry eye on Hercules. "It's a sour day brought *you* to Goody Hall," he grumbled. "Like a cook in a kitchen, the way you stir things up."

But Hercules was full of heroic zeal. He could almost feel the lion skin across his back. "Never mind that," he answered sharply. "The time has come, Mr. Rom, for you to tell what you know. You see, I went down into Midas Goody's tomb last night. He isn't in the coffin. And you're going to tell us about it."

The effect of this speech on Alfresco Rom was remarkable to see. He goggled at Hercules and dropped the trowel he had been holding. His shoulders sagged. And then he turned to Willet and his old black eyes

filled with tears. "I'm glad," he said huskily. "I'm
very glad. It's been a long time to keep a secret." He
reached deep into a pocket of his trousers, pulled up
something, and held it out to Willet. "I promised for
the sake of this," he said. On his calloused palm, like
a drop of dew that sparkled in the sun-dappled doorway of the shed, lay a large diamond. "Now you've
found out, you can have this back. I don't want it any
more. It's been burning me through that pocket for
five years." He closed his fist sharply over the
diamond and then his fingers opened again. The
diamond winked. "I thought I could buy a peaceful
old age with it," he said. "I'm a fool. There's no peace
down that road."

There was a long moment of silence then. Willet
took the diamond and looked at it and put it into his
own pocket. "My mother gave you that diamond,
didn't she?" he asked sadly.

"That she did," said Alfresco in a gentle voice.
"That she did. Come, sit down out here and I'll tell
you all about it."

There was an old wooden bench against the outside wall of the shed. The wisteria grew up and

around it, full and fragrant, from sturdy, twisted roots, a thousand purple blossoms that stirred in the soft breeze. Alfresco sank down on this bench and Willet went to sit cross-legged at his feet. Hercules leaned in the doorway of the shed. He felt that now, somehow, he should stay out of the way.

No one spoke for a while. Alfresco seemed lost in memories. His eyes were vague, as they'd been on the night of the séance, and he gazed out over the lawn to where a large mossy rock lay on the grass warming in the sun. A robin was perched on the rock and it caroled out a string of notes. From the wood at their right, another bird answered cheerily. And then at last Alfresco began to speak.

"It was the garden, mostly, that brought me into it," he said. "Midas Goody came down from the city, ten years ago it is now, and he asked around in the village for land to buy. Settled on this piece here, finally, and wanted it cleared for building. He was a fine man, dressed fine, with plenty of money in his pockets, but he was a shy man, in a way, and his hands were used to work. I saw that right away and I liked him for it. Well, he hired me to clear the land and I did that for him, and then when the house was building, he asked me to stay on to make a garden and care for the lawn. He said he wanted the best garden in the county, and the best house, too. It couldn't be grand enough, he said. A year later, when the house was finished, he came back and brought Mrs. Goody and *you*, lad. You were only a bit of a baby then. And the garden, *my* garden, was just coming to life, too. I loved it. I love it still."

"It's a good garden," said Willet.

Alfresco nodded. "Much obliged. It should be. The roses will be out soon. That's when it's at its best . . . Well, he was kind to me, Midas Goody was, and she was kind to me, too. Your mama. And they took Alfreida to help inside. Everything was fine for a while. And then he took to following me around, after a year or so. 'Here, let *me* do that, Mr. Rom,' he'd say—he never did call me Alfresco—and he'd get down and pull weeds, happy as a crow. One day I asked him, 'How'd you learn to do that, a gentleman like you?' and he said never mind, he just enjoyed it. Well, he seemed to get more and more restless, Midas Goody did, and he took to riding off on his horse, galloping away as if the world was after him."

"What happened to the stable?" asked Hercules. "There must have been a stable."

"She had it tore down. After the accident," said Alfresco. "But wait a bit. I'm coming to that. Then, after about three or four years, he seemed to get very discouraged. The house seemed to bother him. He was hardly ever in it except for meals and sleeping. 'Mr. Rom,' he said to me once, 'that house is a bad thing. I wish I'd never built it.' And that was when he told me how——" Alfresco stopped suddenly and looked down at Willet. "Well, never mind that," he said at last, snapping his old teeth together with a click. "He was hardly ever in that house, as I say, but she, your mama, she loved the house so much she hardly ever went *out* of it." He sighed and wiped his forehead with his handkerchief. "It was along about then he had the tomb built. 'Mr. Rom,' he says to me, 'when Midas Goody dies, he's going to stay right here forever.' He had the tomb built and everything got ready, and that seemed to make him feel better somehow. But not for long. That last year, when you were five, lad, he took to riding off more than ever. And then it happened. It was the day after Pooley's barn burned down. I'd been up to the next village getting some rose cuttings for the garden. I was coming home, nearing evening it was, when I saw him sitting under a tree way down the road. He was just sitting there and the horse was grazing beside him, when all of a sudden, out of the bushes jumps a chor."

"What's a chor?" asked Willet and Hercules both at once.

"Why, a robber," Alfresco explained. "A thief. Well, this chor knocks your father over and grabs the horse, climbs on and goes riding hell for leather down the road before I'm close enough to do a thing to help. But the horse, he doesn't like it much. He knows it's not his master. So all of a sudden he just stops running. Bang. Like that. And the chor goes flying off and whams head first into a tree stump."

"Good lord!" exclaimed Hercules. "What happened then?"

"Well, I was coming along the road as fast as I could but I had those rose cuttings and couldn't go too well. Midas Goody got up and ran down the road to see if the chor was all right, but of course he wasn't. He was dead as a doornail. I could see that, even from where I was, by the funny way he was lying there. Well, Mr. Goody, he stood thinking and then he did such a strange thing that it stopped me in my tracks and sent me into the bushes for cover."

"What did he do?" gasped Willet.

"What he did was he got down and he changed clothes with that chor. Every stitch right down to the shoes and stockings. And then he gets on the horse and rides off across a field and I've never seen him since to this day."

Willet sat with his mouth hanging open in dismay. Hercules, after a moment of stunned silence, said, "Well, go *on*. What happened then?"

"Well," said Alfresco, "I figured he wanted it that way, or he wouldn't have done it, so I didn't call out or anything. I came out of the bushes and I went down the road and looked at the chor all dressed up in Midas Goody's clothes, and along about then, it was nearly dark, a coach comes along and pulls up beside me and a fellow climbs out and says, 'What's the trouble here?' and I says, 'It looks like a horse threw him,' which was nothing but the honest truth. And *he* says, 'I'm a doctor—let me take a look at him,' and he gets down and thumps the chor and pokes at him and then says, 'He's dead. Looks like a broken neck. Do you know where he lives?' And I says, 'Try back down the road there, that big place,' because I figured that's what Midas Goody would have wanted me to say. So the doctor fellow hauls the chor into the coach and they turn around and go back to Goody Hall. By the time *I* get there, it's all over. The doctor has written out the death notice and the chor is in Midas Goody's coffin in the parlor. With the lid closed. And everyone is saying, 'What a shame—poor Mr. Goody's dead.' "

"But what about Mama?" cried Willet. "She must have known it wasn't my father!"

"She knew," said Alfresco. "Of course she knew. And anyway, I went and told her what I'd seen. But she said to me, 'Alfresco,' she says, 'my husband wanted to leave this house. Well, now he's gone and done it. He wanted us all to leave. He never could understand. But this house is Willet's only way to have a good life,' she says, 'and I'm not ever going to leave it. For all anybody'll ever know, Midas Goody's dead.' I said to her, 'How can you tell the boy his father's dead when he isn't?' And she said, 'It's better that Willet should believe his father's dead than—' But then she changed her mind about what she was going to say, and she finished up with 'It's better this way.' So she gave me the diamond and she said, 'It's a secret between us.' And I took it. I've always been sorry."

"But see here," said Hercules. "There's no body in the coffin!"

Alfresco nodded. "That's right," he said. "The very next night, before the funeral, she comes to me and she says, 'Alfresco, we can't put that man in my husband's tomb. I've got so I can't bear the idea. Take him out and bury him somewhere else. I'll put something heavy in the coffin and no one'll ever know the difference.' So that's what I did."

"You buried him somewhere else?" asked Hercules.

"That's right."

"Where?"

"Out there," said Alfresco, pointing to the back

of the lawn. "I put him out there where you see that big rock. It was better than he deserved, at that. Nothing but a chor." They all stared out at the rock. The robin who had been perched there earlier was gone now. "It's got R.I.P. scratched on it somewhere, and a sign of the cross," said Alfresco. "That was the way she wanted it. 'We can't just leave the poor fellow out there with no marker or anything,' she says to me. 'There's worse things than stealing.' She's a good woman in her way." Alfresco sighed heavily. "So that's the way it was, lad. I'm sorry about it all. But at least you know your father's still alive. And it was never you he wanted to leave. Never you, for he loved you dearly." Alfresco stood up and stretched and went to the corner of the shed. He peered around it at the beautiful house, and Willet and Hercules came and stood beside him, looking too. In the sunshine the tiled roofs shone and the windows stared back at them lazily.

"It was that house he wanted to leave," murmured Alfresco. "He didn't like it, never mind he built it himself. And in the end, somehow or other, it drove him away."

Willet started slowly across the lawn, and Hercules followed, and then stopped and came back. "What did Mrs. Goody put into the coffin instead of the . . . the chor?" he asked.

Alfresco shrugged. "I never saw," he answered. "A stone, I suppose."

"It wasn't a statue?" Hercules probed. "A big silver statue of a dog with three heads?"

"A dog with three heads?" said Alfresco. And then, for the first time, he smiled. Like his daughter, Alfreida, he had a gold tooth tucked into a space between his other worn old stumps. The gold tooth winked. "What would she be doing with a dog with three heads?" he said. "No, I never saw anything like that around the place."

"Well, then," said Hercules, "did you ever hear of a man, a thief, named Mott Snave?"

Alfresco smiled again. "Mott Snave? No, I never did. Are you thinking that was the chor's name, maybe?"

"No, I didn't think of that," said Hercules, "although I suppose . . . no, that's very unlikely because . . . well, never mind." He gave it up and went to join Willet. Halfway across the lawn he looked back over his shoulder. Alfresco was watching them still, and still smiling, and the gold tooth winked in the sunlight.

CHAPTER 12

Willet Goody sat beside the iron stag and chewed on the points of his collar. He had been told a hundred times that he mustn't do this because it made the cloth soggy and gray, but he chewed anyway. Beside him, Hercules, in a similar state of distraction, was engrossed in pulling bits of fuzz off the front of his rose-and-dragon vest and stuffing them into the top of one shoe. He plucked and stuffed with the utmost care, and without the least idea he was doing it. There they sat, side by side, chewing and plucking, lost in thought.

After a while Willet stopped chewing and said, "We'll go and look for him."

Hercules stopped plucking. "It's not quite so simple as just up and going off, Willet," he said. "We need some time to figure things out a little. And anyway, we haven't any idea where to look for him."

"That's so," said Willet.

They were silent again. Willet went back to his collar, which was pretty well destroyed by now, for use as a collar, anyway, and Hercules began plucking the vest fuzz out of the first shoe top and stuffing it into the top of the other.

And that is what they were doing when Alfreida turned in at the gate at noon and came up the path toward the house. She stopped when she saw them, and began to laugh, and it wasn't until then that they noticed her. "Well, if that isn't a sight!" she cackled. "I had no idea tutoring was so hard. What's the matter? Can't remember ten times ten?"

Hercules tossed a bit of vest fuzz aside and glared

at her. "Don't laugh, Alfreida. I'm afraid it really isn't very funny."

Alfreida strode across the grass and looked closely at Willet, and her round face sobered. "Oh ho," she said. "So it's like that, is it?" She sat down on Willet's other side and rested her elbows on her knees. "What's the matter, dearie?" she asked in a gentler voice.

"Well," said Willet bravely, "it's a good kind of thing to be the matter, really. I guess there's no harm in telling you, Alfreida. It's about my father. He isn't dead. He only ran away. And now I have to find him."

"Your father isn't dead?" she asked softly.

"No, he isn't. I knew it all along, anyway, and then Hercules went down into the tomb and looked. He isn't in the coffin."

Alfreida looked at Hercules over Willet's head and her little black eyes were bright with satisfaction. "Good for you, dearie," she said. And then she turned back to Willet. "But as for going to find him, what will your mama have to say about that?"

"I don't know," said Willet, "but she isn't here,

anyway. I'm going, and Hercules is coming with me."
He stopped and looked at her. "Alfreida," he said with
a frown, "you don't seem very surprised to hear about
it."

Alfreida gazed across the grass at the garden.
"The daffodils are nearly gone," she said. "Too bad.
They were nice this year."

"Look here, Alfreida," said Hercules. "There was
a big silver statue of Cerberus in Mr. Goody's coffin,
just like the one in the stories you've been telling
Willet. Why did you tell him those stories weren't
true? There really was a thief named Mott Snave,
and heaven knows the statue is real enough."

Alfreida stood up. "I have to go in now," she said.
She started across the grass, and then she stopped
and said over her shoulder, "I said Mott Snave wasn't
a real man, dearie, and I told the truth. He isn't." She
went on to the steps and up to the tall front door of
the beautiful house and then she stopped again,
looked out at them between the pillars, and laughed.
"You're sitting in the right place, anyway, if you're
looking for answers to questions," she called, and disappeared into the house.

They sat staring after her. "I think she knew all about it already," said Willet.

"Maybe," said Hercules, remembering the séance. "Maybe so. It's hard to tell with Alfreida. She never seems surprised at anything."

"What did she mean about sitting in the right place for answering questions?" Willet asked.

"Oh well," said his tutor, "she must be thinking about one of the Hercules stories. One of the ones that's all mixed up with a lot of other stories. He was sent to capture a magic stag once, or a roebuck, anyway. It's the same thing in the stories. The roebuck was sacred to the gods in those days, but he caught it just the same. There are a lot of stories about roebucks, mostly about how if you can follow one, it will lead you to a magic grove of trees, wild apple trees as I remember, where you can learn the answers to all the questions in the world."

Willet sighed. "That would be nice," he said. "Knowing all the answers. I wish our stag could tell us where to look for my father."

"There are a few other questions, you know," said Hercules. "What about the statue in the coffin?

Aren't you curious about that? I know *I* am. And what about the man on the lawn?"

"Well," said Willet, "here's the way I look at it, Hercules. It *is* a funny place to hide a statue . . ."

"It certainly is!" said Hercules.

"But," Willet went on, "I don't really care about that. If Mott Snave wants to hide things in my father's tomb, it's all right with me. *I* don't care. He can hide things down there all day if he wants to. He's probably been looking for years for a good place to put things where that nosy farmer, John Constant, won't find them." Willet stuck out his chin. "Mott Snave can have the whole place, for all I care." He reached into his pocket and pulled out Alfresco's diamond. It lay on his palm, glittering in the sunlight. Willet stared at it for a moment. "He can have this, too," he said, and then he put it back into his pocket again. "No," he said, "I think I'll save it and leave it for my mother. When she comes back and sees it, she'll know we know the whole story and maybe she'll understand why I had to go away." He paused. "You know what I wish, Hercules?"

"What?"

"I wish I could have talked her into coming with us. That would have been so nice, when we find him, to be all together again, wouldn't it?"

The tender heart of Hercules Feltwright gave a wrench and he had to swallow a time or two before he could answer. "Willet," he said at last, "maybe it's not too late. Maybe if you told your mother how you feel, and how you've been worrying all these years—maybe she *would* come along."

Willet Goody glanced across his tutor at the beautiful house and Hercules saw that his eyes were wet. "No," he said in a low voice, "it's no use. I hate that house, but I guess it's pretty important to her somehow. She'll never leave it."

"But Willet, you ought to give her a chance at least," Hercules entreated. "Maybe you're wrong. After all, she probably has no idea you're so unhappy."

"Well," said Willet stoutly, "I didn't want her to know. I didn't want her to feel bad."

"But that's just it!" said Hercules. "You tell me how she's been fooling you, about your father and all, but don't you see, Willet—you've been fooling her, too. Everybody's been fooling everybody all along. Maybe it's time to stop doing that. Maybe you should wait until she comes home and tell her right out how you really feel. Maybe she's unhappy, too. Did you ever think of that? Maybe she *will* come with us and we *can* find your father together."

"Do you really think so, Hercules?"

"I really think you need to try."

Willet rubbed his nose savagely. "All right!" he said. "I will. It's going to be awfully hard, but if you think I should, I will."

Just then a window was thrown open upstairs and the head of a mop was thrust out, flapping and flopping violently. A small cloud of dust motes floated down, silver and shiny in the morning sunlight. They looked up and saw Alfreida's face framed in the window. She smiled down at them. "Just cobwebs, dearies," she called. "The place was full of them."

And then, just before lunchtime, Mrs. Goody came home from the city.

CHAPTER 13

W ell," said Mrs. Tidings, "she's back."

"Ah!" said the blacksmith, moving aside an old horse collar so that his sister could sit down on her customary nail keg. "She's back from the city, is she?"

"That's it," said Mrs. Tidings. She lowered herself onto the keg with a grunt of relief. "She's back, not two hours ago, and Henry, I swear to you, things in that house get queerer by the minute."

The blacksmith took out his pipe and filled and lit it happily. "You don't say so!" he said, between puffs. He clamped his teeth around the pipe stem, pulled up his own nail keg, and sat, leaning toward her.

These preliminaries having been completed, Mrs. Tidings folded her arms under her large bosom and began on the main business. "Yes, she's back, and not a package on her anywhere. *As* usual."

The blacksmith, picking up his cue, nodded and echoed, "As usual."

"*But*—" said Mrs. Tidings, "never mind that. We expected that. What we didn't expect was this: I told her about that strange visitor of Mr. Feltwright's and about Mr. Feltwright's inheritance and all, and that didn't seem to interest her at all."

"Hmmm!" said the blacksmith.

"That is to *say*," said Mrs. Tidings, building suspense carefully, "that is to *say*, Henry, it didn't interest her until I told her the *name* of Mr. Feltwright's visitor—you remember, Mott Snave it was. When I told her that, Henry, she turned white as a sheet. 'You must have made a mistake,' she said, and *I* said, 'No mistake about it, that was the fellow's name.' And *she* said, 'How was he dressed?' and when I told her, you know, about the cloak and the scarf, and how he'd even been seen here, in the village, she sat down, all of a sudden like, as if her knees had given out."

"Bless my soul!" said the blacksmith. "Then she's heard of him before, that's clear enough."

"Well, of course she has!" said Mrs. Tidings triumphantly. "Have you seen him at all since that first time?"

"No," said the blacksmith with obvious disappointment. "Not hide nor hair."

"Hmmm," said Mrs. Tidings. She was silent for a moment. The blacksmith puffed away on his pipe and waited. "Henry," she said at last, "I have this feeling —it's just a feeling, mind you—I have this definite feeling that something's going to happen."

The blacksmith took his pipe out of his mouth and nodded vigorously. "I've had the same feeling, Dora," he said excitedly. "I've felt that way for days."

"Well, whatever it is that happens," said Mrs.

Tidings, "if anything *does* happen, I hope I'm there to see it. I've known all along, right from the very beginning, that there was something wrong out to Goody Hall, and I guess I've said as much to you a time or two." She looked at her brother with smug expectancy.

He didn't disappoint her. "Indeed you have, Dora," he nodded. "Time and again you've said so, and who's to disagree?"

"Exactly," said Mrs. Tidings. And then she repeated, "I hope I'm there to see it. If anything *does* happen."

"You've earned that much anyway, Dora, it seems to me," said the blacksmith. "It's strange, all right. I've had that same feeling for days. Something's going to happen."

CHAPTER 14

Mrs. Goody stayed in her room all afternoon—
"She's resting," Alfreida explained—and
then came down to dinner in a rich dress of yellow
silk with a wide lace collar. Her hair was piled high
on her head and there was a small feather fastened
into the intricate loops and curls. But her face was
pale and she kept plucking nervously at the collar. Alfreida, who was serving the meal, moved in and out

of the dining room silently, and Hercules remembered how Willet had said she was always silent when his mother was at home. But he watched her face and thought to himself that her eyes, when she glanced at Mrs. Goody, were sympathetic.

Unlike Alfreida, Mrs. Goody seemed anxious to talk. "Well, my love," she said a little breathlessly to Willet, "how did you get along while I was gone?"

"Fine, Mama, just fine," said Willet guardedly.

"Did you start your lessons with Mr. Feltwright?"

"Well, pretty much," said Willet.

"We spent some time on nature," said Hercules hastily, hoping she wouldn't think he had been entirely idle. "Birds and flowers. And we worked on spelling, too."

Mrs. Goody nodded. "That sounds like a good beginning."

Silence.

"It rained the night before last," Hercules offered.

"Yes, it rained in the city, too," said Mrs. Goody.

"But no thunder and lightning," said Hercules.

"No, that's true. Just rain."

The conversation lagged again. All three searched

their minds for something to say. Hercules Feltwright
felt the press of his own knowledge weighting his
tongue, and knew that Willet was feeling the same
way. And it was clear that Mrs. Goody was agitated
by some knowledge of her own. She kept glancing at
Hercules and then glancing quickly away. Then,
they all spoke at once.

"How were things in the . . ."

"Those lilacs outside my . . ."

"I understand, Mr. Feltwright, that . . ."

All three paused. At last Mrs. Goody smiled faintly
and took up the thread of her own remark. "I understand, Mr. Feltwright, that you were once an actor."

"Oh, yes!" he answered with relief. Here was a
safe subject. "Not so long ago. We toured the countryside with all sorts of plays."

"I used to go to plays from time to time when I
was a girl," said Mrs. Goody. "It was always such a
pleasure."

"How come you never took *me* to see one?" asked
Willet accusingly.

"But, Willet!" she said. "There wasn't any you
when I was a girl, you know, and after we came here,

no troupes ever came by. I would have had to take you off somewhere else and I just didn't want—that is, I didn't think it would . . ." Her voice trailed off and she glanced at Hercules again. Not such a safe subject after all, he thought to himself, feeling puzzled and curious.

Then, when dinner was nearly over, and after a good many more stops and starts in the conversation, Mrs. Goody put down her fork suddenly and looked hard at Hercules. "Where is your home, Mr. Feltwright?" she asked him.

"Why, north of here," he answered, a little surprised. "About a hundred miles north."

"A hundred miles north," Mrs. Goody echoed. Her shoulders sagged. She stared at him and then looked away and added, in a more normal tone, "Mrs. Tidings tells me you stand to inherit a fortune from an old aunt."

Hercules Feltwright blushed. "Look here, Mrs. Goody," he said, putting down his own fork. "That was a misunderstanding that's gotten out of hand. I do have an aunt, but she's not rich by any means, quite the opposite, and I don't expect to inherit anything but a box of broken pennies. I'm glad you brought it up because I've been feeling bad about the whole business. If there's anything in the world I don't want, it's to have people think I'm anything but what I really am."

Mrs. Goody's face went pink. "You needn't have said that!" she cried. "It wasn't really like that."

Now it was Hercules Feltwright's turn to stare. "W-why, I only meant," he stammered, "that it's important to me to be . . . uh . . . well, not to pretend, you know. That is to say . . ."

"Never mind," said Mrs. Goody flatly. "I take your meaning." Her eyes were anguished as she looked at him. "You're very young, Mr. Feltwright. You have no right to judge, even if he did send you here. Sometimes people have to pretend in order to get what they want."

"But, Mrs. Goody!" Hercules protested. "I don't understand! I wasn't trying to say—I mean, I didn't have in mind anything to do with . . ."

"Never mind," she said again. "Tell me—what was the name of the town where you lived, a hundred miles north?"

"Why, Hackston Fen," he answered, more baffled than ever.

"I see," said Mrs. Goody. "Of course. Hackston Fen." She put down her napkin, looked at Willet, plucked again at her collar, and then, all at once, she pressed her palms against her cheeks and smiled, but only for an instant. The smile faded as quickly as it had come, and when she spoke again, her voice was sober. "Well," she said. "It seems we'd better have a little talk, the three of us. Something's going to happen soon. Mrs. Tidings told me that someone . . . well, something may happen, and before it does there are a lot of things I want to explain, because . . . Well, come along. We'll go upstairs now." She stood and went quickly around the table to Willet's chair. "Come, my love," she said to him. "You're the one it's really all about." And she bent and gave him a swift hug.

"That's all right, Mama," said Willet.

In Willet's room the evening light was gold and blue. On their shelves, the rows and rows of elegant toys stood silent. Mrs. Goody, sitting near them in a wicker rocker, reached out and picked up a big stuffed dog made of white plush. "You know," she said suddenly, stroking it, "I had a real dog when I was a girl."

"You *did?*" said Willet incredulously. "I didn't know that. Didn't your mother mind about the hairs on the furniture and digging up the flowers?"

"No," said Mrs. Goody with a little smile. "She didn't mind."

"I had a dog, too," said Hercules, suddenly misty-eyed. "A little dog with brown spots that used to bite peddlers."

But Mrs. Goody didn't seem to hear him. Still holding the plush dog, she got up from the rocker and went to the window and peered out. After a moment she straightened, sighed, and came back to sit down again. "You have to understand, Willet," she said at last, "that I was never rich in those days."

"You weren't? I didn't know that," said Willet again.

"I lived on a farm, you see," said Mrs. Goody.

"We had the oldest of furniture. And the flowers all grew wild except for the pansies in a garden I planted myself."

"You had your own garden?" said Willet. "Oh, that must have been nice."

"Well, yes—it was," said Mrs. Goody. "Yes, I liked it. I haven't thought about that garden for years, but now . . . yes, it *was* nice. But we all worked very hard, you see, Willet. My father was a farmer and he was in the fields all day from early spring to the end of autumn. I can see him now, going up and down, up and down behind the horse . . ."

"What kind of horse?" asked Willet.

"Oh, not a fancy horse like your father's," she said. "An old, strong, kindly horse with big hooves. He was—I remember him so well—he had a soft nose and he used to nuzzle in your hand when you fed him sugar."

"I never fed a horse any sugar," said Willet. "It sounds like fun."

"Well, it was, I suppose. Yes, of course it was. Although, I always liked the little animals best, the baby lambs and the new little pigs, and . . . But,

Willet, the thing I want you to understand is that we worked very hard. I used to help my mother bake the bread, you know. It had a smell that . . . Well. But I cleaned the house and helped with the washing and then in the winter we used to have to keep a big fire going in the stove. I can remember how I used to warm my toes on it, and sometimes we would . . . But, Willet. Don't you see? My mother grew old in that kitchen, and my father grew old in the fields."

"Didn't they like living on the farm?" asked Willet. "Were they very unhappy?"

"Why . . ." said Mrs. Goody, "I suppose they were happy enough. I didn't think about that at the time. My father used to play the fiddle. He played it on winter evenings mostly, when he had more time. We used to dance round and round the stove and I remember once . . ." Then she stopped and the warmth that had lit her face died away. "Willet, it seemed like a hard life. Hard work. You can't imagine, living in this house."

"Maybe it was hard," said Willet, "but you sound as if you liked it anyway, Mama. Your own dog, and the garden and the fiddle and all."

Mrs. Goody looked away. "Well, anyway," she said with a sigh, "when we built this house, your father and I, I knew I had left that life behind forever. That my child—*you*, my love—could live with beautiful things and have the best of everything always. I wanted it that way. We built this house to match all our dreams, dreams for ourselves and *you*. I did so want you to be happy."

There was a long silence then. Finally, Willet drew a deep breath and Hercules, sitting on the bed beside him, felt him tremble. He reached into his pocket and pulled out the diamond. "Hercules went down into the tomb, Mama," he said. "My father isn't down there. And then Alfresco told us all about everything. He isn't dead at all. He only ran away. I knew he wasn't dead, Mama. I always knew it. And I want to go and look for him. Hercules is coming with me, and—I want you to come, too, because . . ." His voice faltered. Hercules took his hand and squeezed it, and after a moment got an answering squeeze. "Because," Willet went on at last, "I hate this house and the way we have to live in it. I'm sorry, Mama, if you wanted it for me. I'm really sorry. But—I don't want it. I don't like anything about it and—I want to go away."

Mrs. Goody's face went white. She clutched the plush dog to her breast as if it were the only thing that could keep her upright. "What do you mean?" she gasped at last, her voice faint with shock. All at once she sat forward in the rocker, every muscle rigid, and her eyes flashed. "That's nonsense!" she cried. "Nothing but nonsense. You're only a child. How could you possibly know what's best for you? This is the only kind of life worth living. How can you say you don't want it, you foolish boy? Why, this is the most beautiful house in the world! And it's full of beautiful things. And you have all these toys and fine clothes to wear, and a tutor, and . . . Why, I've given up everything for this, do you hear me? I've given up everything!" She stopped. The words hung in the air like the sound of a slap: I've given up everything.

As if she were hearing them for the first time, those words that said so much, as if she had been struck by them, Mrs. Goody's eyes widened and the plush dog dropped from her arms and tumbled to the floor.

She stared blankly at Willet. From the bed, Willet stared back at her through a shimmering haze of tears. He was scarcely breathing, and had so tight a grip on his tutor's hand that Hercules would have winced but for the fact that he was numb with all-consuming hope.

At last the wrenching moment passed. Mrs. Goody shook her head in slow and gentle wonder. "Dear heaven!" she whispered. "What am I saying? But no—it's true. And more than that, I've known it all along. I *have* given up everything, in order to have —all this. I kept telling myself that beautiful things —they're supposed to make you happy, aren't they? But when you try to warm yourself beside them, you see how cold they are. I found that out after your father went away, but I never let myself admit it. Yes, I gave up everything and that means I have nothing left, that I've given you—nothing. And here I sit like an idiot, expecting you to be grateful."

There was silence again in the room, but it was a new kind of silence that seemed to quiver. From somewhere outside the window, a bird called to its mate in a lonely fragment of song that filled the evening for a moment with sad and piercing sweetness and then was hushed. And the crickets, as if the song of the bird had been a signal, took over at once in their own way with their own crisp, rasping song that softened the edges of the silence in Willet's room as sandpaper softens wood. The three sat quietly, listening, and then at last Mrs. Goody stirred. "Oh, Willet," she said heavily. "Willet. What a *waste*. All those years, my love, all those long and empty years." She leaned back in the rocker and her eyes closed.

Outside the window, over the music of the crickets, the solitary bird called once again. But this time, from farther away, there was an answering snatch of song, a bright, clear string of joyful notes that spilled suddenly into the dusk as from a small heart too full to hold them. Mrs. Goody opened her eyes and the pain that had dulled them was gone. She sat up. "But—Willet!" she cried. "This means that—why, it's over, Willet! It's *over!* We don't have to pretend any more, not ever. Oh, my love, my dear child, all these years I've been shoving my doubts aside, never

looking at them squarely, because I thought that you
—but you never wanted it in the first place! You
never wanted it at all! So—we're *free!*"

She sprang up and went to the window again, and
when she came back to the rocker, her step was quick
and light. "My dears," she said, "I am a fool! No,
don't say it isn't so. I am. A perfect fool. Imagine ever
trying to believe that anything so cold and . . . stiff
as all this"—and her sweeping gesture included the
room where they sat, included the entire house—
"anything so cold and stiff as *this*"—bending over
and seizing the plush dog, holding it up and making
a face at it—"could possibly stuff up the chinks and
stop the drafts in a life all full of holes. You knew it
couldn't, didn't you, Willet, all by yourself. But now
—oh, *Willet*, now we *can* go back. At last! And we
will. All together." At the thought of this her cheeks
grew pink and she turned to Hercules with a sudden
smile of excitement. "To think that you know him,
Mr. Feltwright! To think he came here while I was
away and asked for you! Mrs. Tidings told me all
about it. He sent you to us, didn't he?"

Hercules stared at her. "But . . . no! No, Mrs. Goody! I didn't . . . that wasn't . . ."

But Mrs. Goody wasn't listening. "Every year, twice a year, since the night he went away, I've gone up to the city and I've sold off the jewels one by one to keep things going—after all, the bishop did say whoever could steal them could keep them. Your father, Willet, he did what he felt *he* had to do—he went back and told the whole story. They put him in jail, of course. It wasn't really his fault that the bishop tripped and fell into that well, but then, of course, it wouldn't have happened if he hadn't been there for the bishop to chase, so in a way he was responsible. Well, you know all about it already. It's so strange —I was going to explain everything tonight. He'd been here, and Mr. Feltwright knows him, so it seemed to me that the time had come—but here Alfresco has told it all first. Well, it doesn't matter now, thank goodness. Only, I hope he's all right. A five-year term they gave him! That's a long time. I asked Alfresco to write once, you see. Did he tell you that? Five years! I knew it would happen that way and I didn't want you to know your father was in jail. Thinking he was dead seemed better than that. But now—I'm *proud* of him!" she said with sudden fierceness. "It was foolish, all that dressing up and stealing things, and then taking them back like that, just for the excitement. He was a farmer, too, you know, Willet, just like my father, but he was so young and eager for adventure, and it wasn't until after we were married that I knew about it, anyway. The statue was to have been the last time—a kind of glorious ending —and then he was going to put away that second life forever. But, instead, the bishop drowned and there was no one to take the statue back to, and all of a sudden, when we found it was full of jewels, a third life hung there just waiting to be plucked. To be rich! And easy! Happiness. But it wasn't. Not for him. That statue opened the Gates of Hell for him. It had three heads, he used to say, just as he did. And he couldn't go on pretending. And after—after he went away, I put it in the coffin so I'd never have to look at it again. But now—it's all over! I see what a terrible fool I was to cling to it so long, and he—well, I won't argue with him ever again when he . . . but hush! What was that?" She held up a hand, and her eyes, shining with unshed tears, went watchful.

The two mouths of the two on the bed had been slowly dropping open. "Do you mean to say, Mrs. Goody," gasped Hercules when she paused, "that Midas Goody is really . . ."

"Hackston Fen!" said Mrs. Goody. "He bought the hat from a hatter there. It will be so good to see Hackston Fen again. Not five miles from the farm, it is. And, oh, Willet, it will be lovely to be our own true selves again . . . but hush! Don't you hear something?"

They listened. From the end of the hall came a dull thump.

"What was that?" Mrs. Goody whispered. The thump came again, and after it the unmistakable sound of a window being opened. Mrs. Goody sprang up. "Come!" she cried. "Come quickly! I think—I think it's happening." She ran out of the room and down the hall, and Willet and Hercules ran after her. At the door of her bedroom they all stopped and peered in. There before them, climbing in through an open window in the blue glow of dusk, was a man in black cloak and flat black hat, a man whose face was nearly covered by a winding of long red scarf. Hearing them, he jerked up his head and the scarf pulled away from his face. "Ye gods!" he said. "You startled me! Hello, my loves. I've come to take you home."

"Mott Snave!" gasped Hercules.

"But it isn't!" shouted Willet joyfully. "It's my very own father! It's Midas Goody!"

And Mrs. Goody, laughing and weeping both at once, flung out her arms. "Oh, John!" she cried. "John Constant! You've come back at last!"

CHAPTER 15

Reunions in those long gone times were exactly like reunions today, of course. Some things never change. The mood was just as merry, the smiles as tender, and the air had that same expansive lightness which threatened, if you breathed too deeply, to lift you right up off the floor. Hercules Feltwright, embarrassed but pleased, stood apart and drank in borrowed joy, and all at once, with all his soul, he

longed for a reunion of his own. The charms of
Hackston Fen, so long neglected, rose up in his
memory like a siren's song, sweet and irresistible.
"I'll go home, too," he promised himself. "Not to be a
hatter or a hero or anything foolish, but home, never-
theless. Why, I'll go home and—start a school, that's
what I'll do! The Hackston Fen Academy. Or—no.
I'll call it The Feltwright School of Thought and I'll
teach . . ." He paused and blushed in the sudden
realization that everyone was looking at him curiously.

"Wake up, Hercules!" said Willet, laughing. "I've
said it twice already—come here and meet my father."

He was, this father of Willet's, exactly as Alfresco
had described him—a big man, a fine man, with
hands that were used to work. And he did indeed have
a large nose, which now, with the emotion of the
moment, he was forced to blow from time to time
with an enormous white handkerchief. His yellow
beard, trim and full, was so splendid that the blacksmith himself might have envied it. Hercules eyed
the beard and, rubbing his own undecorated chin
reflectively, wondered if perhaps he might not try one

after all. Just to see how it would look. But more than
the beard and the nose, he admired the plain delight
of this man who had been away so long, the pride in
his eyes when he looked at his son, and looked and
looked at him, and the eager, grateful clasp of his
arm about the shoulder of his wife. "How do you do,
Mr. Goody," said Hercules with satisfaction. "I mean,
Mr. Snave. No, it's Mr. Constant, isn't it?"

"I'm glad to meet you, Mr. Feltwright," beamed
Willet's father. "Very glad indeed. And Constant is
my name—Constant to begin with and Constant from
now on."

"Never mind pretending, John," said Mrs. Goody
with a severity that her happy face belied. "We know
you two have met before. We know all about it."

This, of course, brought on a long series of expla-
nations, full of interruptions and laughter and such
confusion that some things had to be repeated a
number of times before everyone understood. For it
was quite true: Hercules and John Constant had
indeed met before—there on the lawn in the dark,
each in his cape, hat, and scarf—though neither of
them had realized it at the time, and this, in the tell-

ing, caused more confusion and laughter than anything else. But at last it was all made clear, the last of the tangled webs was swept away, and John Constant sank into a chair with his wife and son at his feet. Hercules, who had been told a number of times that he must stay, that he was part of it all, leaned against a bedpost and looked on, aware that he was as pleased as he'd ever been in all his life; pleased with himself, pleased with the three before him, pleased, even, with his mother and father and every soul in Hackston Fen. "In a queer kind of way," he said to himself, "it's fitting for me to go home now. The last Labor of Hercules is finished. I've gone down to the Gates of Hell and I've come to grips with Cerberus, and it's all over. Even my mother should see that." And so he stayed and leaned and listened, and was supremely content.

"I've been in jail, you know, my loves," John Constant was saying soberly.

"We know, John," said Mrs. Goody. "And we're proud of you."

"I went back to the farm the moment I was free," he went on. "It will take a great deal of work to get it going again, I'm afraid. But—I couldn't wait. I've missed you so. I got out the old Mott Snave costume and came down here at once, to see if I could talk you into coming home."

"Are you going to start being Mott Snave again, Father?" asked Willet.

"Ye gods! Certainly not!" said John Constant. "That's over forever. It's just that I knew if anyone here were to see me as myself, it would cause all sorts of ruckus. Why, can't you imagine what Mrs. Tidings would have done if I'd just walked up to the door?"

"She'd have fainted dead away," said Mrs. Goody, "or worse."

"Exactly," said John Constant. "So I put on the costume and I climbed in through the window so I could meet you again up here, my loves, without any questions or interruptions or people peeking around corners. I came three days ago, as a matter of fact, and I've been sneaking about like a regular cutpurse, scared to death I'd be recognized. Where were you, my dear? I was afraid perhaps you'd gone away for good."

"I was in the city, John," his wife explained. "Selling off another of the jewels."

"Oh. Yes," he sighed. "You've had to do that, of course. Yes, there wasn't any other way. But we'll leave the rest of those jewels behind, and the statue, too. For the church, perhaps—that would be best. In a way, it's where they came from. That is—" he looked at her anxiously, "if you're willing, if you're ready to come. Are you? Will you come back to the farm with me, you and Willet? We can get it going again, the three of us; we can do it together. Will you come home?"

Mrs. Goody's eyes were too bright to tease him successfully, but she tried anyway. She pursed her lips. "We-ell, John, I don't know. I don't see how we can, really, when there isn't so much as a single dog anywhere about up there."

"We'll get a dog!" boomed John Constant joyfully. "We'll get two! Three, if it will bring you home any faster."

"Very well, John," she said primly. "Then the answer is yes. We'll come home."

"Oh!" cried Willet. "A real dog? For me?"

"Yes, my love," said his mother emphatically, throwing her arms around him and drawing him close. "A real dog, and a garden too, where you can dig and get dirty and plant anything you like. We'll have it all, except for the fiddle. I'm afraid I never learned to play the fiddle."

Willet looked at Hercules over his mother's arm and gave him a blinding smile. "That's all right, Mama," he said.

CHAPTER 16

"Dora!" said the blacksmith in great surprise as his sister puffed into the shop next morning. "Dora, what's the matter? What are you doing with all those bundles? Why, bless my soul! Isn't that your work basket? And your clothes? *All* your clothes?"

Mrs. Tidings dropped her bundles on the floor of the shop. She stood there with an expression of mingled regret, delight, and anger on her plump face. "Henry," she said slowly, "Henry, you'll never believe it. I've been sacked, Henry. Mrs. Goody has let me go."

The blacksmith stared. "What are you saying, Dora?" he cried. "Sacked? Why? What did you do?"

"Ah!" said Mrs. Tidings with deep satisfaction. "It isn't what *I* did, Henry. Not what *I* did. It's what *she* did."

"Tell me! Tell me!" said the blacksmith.

Mrs. Tidings folded her arms. "That woman is beyond shame, Henry. I guarantee you won't believe it. She's running off with the fellow in the cloak and scarf."

"That fellow Snave?" gasped the blacksmith.

"The very one," replied his sister. "It was the queerest thing I ever saw. I heard a noise in the middle of the night and I went out into the hall and there was young Feltwright coming in the front door with a big statue in his arms—a statue of a dog with three heads. I heard him go up the stairs and he went into her bedroom with it and shut the door. After a while I heard laughing and someone said, 'One head is enough for anyone.' I went up and knocked on her door. She opened it, not right away, but she opened it, and there they all were, she and Mr. Feltwright and Master Willet and that fellow Snave with that scarf pulled up over his face. And she said to me that she wouldn't be needing me any longer because they were going away in the morning."

The blacksmith sank down on a nail keg and pulled at his beard. "To think she'd leave that house!" he goggled.

"More than that, Henry, she's running off and leaving her poor husband all alone in his tomb with no one to look after him. That's the real scandal, right there."

"That's so, I hadn't thought of that," said the blacksmith. "Are you sure about all this, Dora? It seems impossible."

"Well, of course I'm sure! They were just about to leave when I came away this morning. I didn't see Snave, but she was in the kitchen, singing like a lark, making a picnic for breakfast. Imagine her in a kitchen! And a picnic. For *breakfast!*"

They stared at each other, torn between astonishment and delight. And then Mrs. Tidings said, "She told me to give a message to that gypsy gardener. She said I was to tell him he should keep the garden for himself. I asked her, I said, 'What about the house?' But she only said, 'Never mind the house.' " Mrs. Tidings shook her head helplessly and sighed.

"But what about that tutor fellow?" asked the blacksmith. "What's to become of him?"

Mrs. Tidings blushed to the roots of her hair. "Henry," she said, "he kissed me. I was just about to go out the door this morning when there was a terrible rumpus upstairs and then here came Master Willet sliding down the banister. With young Feltwright just behind him. Sliding down the *banister*, Henry. And he bounced up to me and flung his arms around me and gave me a kiss on the forehead."

"He kissed you?" gasped the blacksmith.

"He did! And he said, '*Good*bye, Dora, I'm going home.' And Master Willet said, 'He's going to start a school, Mrs. Tidings. Kiss her again, Hercules!' And he *did*, Henry. He *did!*" She blushed again and beamed, caught herself and quickly assumed a very severe expression. "Imagine! Such behavior!"

"Well," said the blacksmith faintly, "we knew something was going to happen. We both felt it."

Just at that moment someone screamed outside the shop. Instantly, there were shouts and the sound of running feet. Mrs. Tidings and the blacksmith hurried to the door. "Bless my soul!" cried Mrs. Tidings. "Look up there! Isn't that Millie, the baker's daughter?" And she pointed to the roof of the church which stood across the street. There, near the steeple, a figure was teetering on the eaves, the slim figure of a girl with her hands pressed to her heart. In the street below, a large crowd was gathering and everyone was shouting and gesturing.

"Don't do it, Millie!"

"Don't jump, child! No man is worth that, not even a parson!"

"Do something, somebody!"

And the girl, in between the shouts of the crowd, was making quite a noise of her own. "If I can't have the parson," she shrieked, "I can't go on living! Goodbye, dear friends! Goodbye!" And at last, as a mighty gasp went up from the crowd, the girl flung up her arms, wailed one last tragic farewell, and leaped out into space. Down she plummeted like a stone, and landed squarely on top of the poor parson, who was hovering below, wringing his hands.

After a moment of hushed silence, someone yelled, "She's all right!"

"But the parson isn't," yelled another. "Looks like his leg is broken. Get a doctor, someone!"

And then, as the crowd ran hither and thither looking for the doctor, a new cry went up from the end of the street and the terrible cracking boom of a shot rang out.

"Whee-ow!" cried the blacksmith, quite purple with excitement. "It's Fred Hulser! He's escaping from jail!"

And it was. Down the street a snorting horse came galloping at a great rate, and on its back clung a thin, desperate figure brandishing a pistol.

"Stop him!" everyone yelled, scattering to make room for the speeding horse. "Stop him! Cow thief!"

"No, no!" cried one lone voice. "Let him go! Run, Fred! Run, son!"

"It's his father! It's Alf!" someone shouted. "Go to it, Alf!"

The blacksmith was jumping up and down, beside himself, and Mrs. Tidings had rushed out into the street in order to see better. The village was in turmoil. "Hurry, everyone!" a commanding voice called. "After him! *After* him!"

And then, just as the crowd was organizing to rush after poor Fred Hulser, a new and final cry went up. "Look! *Look!* Smoke! Back that way!"

"Hurray!" bellowed the blacksmith, hoarse with joy. "It's Pooley's barn, right on schedule!"

Millie, the parson, Fred Hulser, all were forgotten in an instant. The crowd swung around, and away they all ran, Mrs. Tidings and the blacksmith with the rest. "It's Pooley's barn, Dora!" cried the blacksmith to his sister. "It's burning down again, five years almost to the minute!" He pounded along, his mouth hanging open in a loose and gasping grin.

"What a day!" puffed Mrs. Tidings, bouncing and leaping beside him. "What a *day!*"

Down the road they ran pell-mell, toward the billowing black smoke that rolled up above the trees and hung in the sky, filling the air with the sharp, rich smell of scorching wood. Now and then a shower of

sparks shot up and, whenever this happened, a delighted yell rose from the crowd and they ran even
faster.

And then they slowed, faltered, came to a halt.
They had arrived at Pooley's barn. It stood there calm
and peaceful and intact beside the road. A curious pig
emerged from its cool interior and regarded them
with interest. There wasn't so much as an ember in
sight.

"Good heavens!" cried Mrs. Tidings suddenly. "If
it isn't Pooley's barn, then it must be . . . oh, it
couldn't be, could it?"

But it could. Oh yes, it could. They began to run
again, past Pooley's barn and on down the road for
another mile, around a sudden bend where one short
week ago a baggy young man had strolled, swinging
his battered satchel and singing. And here, like him,
they stopped. There before them, on its dewy square
of barbered lawn, Goody Hall rose up like a giant
torch, engulfed in flames. The heat was immense.
As they watched in shock and amazement, one peaking turret began to topple. Down it crashed in a roar
of sparks and smoke. And soon the entire roof began

to sag, to buckle. Slowly, tantalizingly, it sank inward and collapsed.

"Is there anyone in there?" someone asked in an awed voice.

"No, dearie," came the answer from a round little woman with a gold tooth. Alfreida Rom leaned on the gate and watched as Goody Hall blazed away into ashes, and her voice was gentle with finality and satisfaction. "No, dearie," she said, "there's no one in there. They've all gone away."

"But where did they go?" asked someone else.

Alfreida smiled. "They went back," she answered. "*And* on. To better things."

GOFISH

What did you want to be when you grew up?
When I was a preschooler, I wanted to be a pirate, and then when I started school, I wanted to be a librarian. But in the fourth grade, I got my copy of *Alice in Wonderland / Alice Through the Looking-Glass* and decided once and for all that I wanted to be an illustrator of stories for children.

When did you realize you wanted to be a writer?
I didn't even think about writing. My husband wrote the story for the first book. But then he didn't want to do it anymore, so I had to start writing my own stories. After

all, you can't make pictures for stories unless you have stories to make pictures for.

What's your first childhood memory?
I have a lot of preschool memories, all from when we lived in a little town just south of Columbus, Ohio. I kind of remember sitting in a high chair. And when I was a little older, I remember seeing Jack Frost looking in through the kitchen window. *That* was pretty surprising.

What's your most embarrassing childhood memory?
I don't remember any. I'm probably just suppressing them all.

What's your favorite childhood memory?
I think I liked best the times when my sister and I would curl up next to our mother while she read aloud to us.

As a young person, who did you look up to most?
No question: my mother.

What was your worst subject in school?
Arithmetic. I think you call it math now.

What was your best subject in school?
Art. And after that, English.

What was your first job?

It was when I was a teenager. I worked in what we called the College Shop in a big downtown Cleveland (Ohio) department store called Higbee's. But after that, I mostly worked in the pricing department of a washing machine factory.

How did you celebrate publishing your first book?

I don't think I did anything special. By that time, I was beginning to get over my absolute astonishment at having found my editor in the *first* place. That was the most wonderful moment of all.

Where do you write your books?

I think about them for a long time before I actually start putting words on paper, and I think about them all over the place. Then, when I'm ready, I work at my computer in my workroom. But before, I always wrote them out longhand, sitting on my sofa in the living room. I wrote on a big tablet, and then I typed everything, paragraph by paragraph, on my typewriter, making changes as I went along.

Where do you find inspiration for your writing?

I mostly write about all the unanswered questions I still have from when I was in elementary school.

Which of your characters is most like you?
The main characters in all of my long stories are like me, but I think Winnie Foster, in *Tuck Everlasting,* is most like me.

When you finish a book, who reads it first?
Always my editor, Michael di Capua. His opinion is the most important one.

Are you a morning person or a night owl?
Neither one, really. I'm mostly a middle-of-the-day person.

What's your idea of the best meal ever?
One that someone else cooked. And it has to have something chocolate for dessert.

Which do you like better: cats or dogs?
Cats to look at and to watch, but dogs to own.

What do you value most in your friends?
Good talk and plenty of laughing.

Where do you go for peace and quiet?
Now that my children are grown and gone into lives of their own, I have plenty of peace and quiet just sitting around the house.

What makes you laugh out loud?
Words. My father was very funny with words, and I grew up laughing at the things he said.

What's your favorite song?
Too many to mention, but most of them are from the '30s and '40s, when songs were to *sing*, not to shout and wiggle to.

Who is your favorite fictional character?
No question: Alice from *Alice in Wonderland* and *Alice Through the Looking-Glass.*

What are you most afraid of?
I have a fear that is very common when we are little, and I seem to have hung on to it: the fear of being abandoned.

What time of year do you like best?
May is my favorite month.

What is your favorite TV show?
I don't watch many shows anymore—just CNN News and old movies.

If you were stranded on a desert island, who would you want for company?
My husband, Sam.

If you could travel in time, where would you go?
Back to Middletown, Ohio, to Lincoln School on Central Avenue, to live through fifth grade again. And again and again.

What's the best advice you have ever received about writing?
No one single thing. Too many good things to list.

What do you want readers to remember about your books?
The questions without answers.

What would you do if you ever stopped writing?
Spend all my time doing word puzzles and games, and practicing the good old songs on my piano.

What do you like best about yourself?
That I can draw, and play the good old songs on my piano.

What is your worst habit?
Always expecting things to be perfect.

What is your best habit?
Trying to make things as perfect as I can.

What do you consider to be your greatest accomplishment?
Right now, it's a picture for a new book that hasn't even been published yet. It's a picture of a man in a washtub, floating on the ocean in a rainstorm. I'm really proud of that picture.

Where in the world do you feel most at home?
That's a hard question. My family moved away from Middletown, Ohio (see the question/answer about time travel), when I was in the middle of sixth grade, and we never went back. Even after all these years, though, Middletown is the place I think of when I think about "home." I've lived in a lot of different places, though, and liked them all, so I don't feel sorry for myself. It's just that the word "home" has its own kind of special meaning.

What do you wish you could do better?
Everything. Cook, write, play the piano, everything.

What would your readers be most surprised to learn about you?
Maybe that I believe that writing books is a long way from being important. The most important thing anyone can do is be a teacher. As for those of us who write books, I often think we should all stop for fifty years. There are so many wonderful books to read, and not

enough time to get around to all of them. But we writers just keep cranking them out. All we can hope for is that readers will find at least a little time for them, anyway.

SQUARE FISH